Sheet Sahasik Hemantolok

OXFORD NOVELLAS
Encompassing literature, popular and genre fiction,
writers old and new, this series presents an orchestra
of Indic voices

Series Editor: Mini Krishnan

Other titles in the Series

Sheet Sahasik Hemantolok
Defying Winter

Nabaneeta Dev Sen

Translated from Bengali by
Tutun Mukherjee

OXFORD
UNIVERSITY PRESS

OXFORD
UNIVERSITY PRESS

Oxford University Press is a department of the University of Oxford.
It furthers the University's objective of excellence in research,scholarship,
and education by publishing worldwide. Oxford is a registered trademark of
Oxford University Press in the UK and in certain other countries

Published in India by
Oxford University Press
YMCA Library Building, 1 Jai Singh Road, New Delhi 110 001, India

ISBN-13: 978-0-19-809743-3
ISBN-10: 0-19-809743-3

Typeset in Berling LT Std 10/15.5,
at MAP Systems, Bengaluru 560 082, India
Printed in India at Akash Press, New Delhi 110 020

To
The lonely and insecure women in
old age homes in India who have let their
beauty turn inward ...

CONTENTS

Series Editor's Note

*'Freedom is knowing and understanding things
quite other than ourselves.'*

–Anonymous

Writers have always experimented with forms in their search
for the best vehicles for their thoughts, moods, and words.
While there might be arguments about what length defines
the genre, the novella was shaped and recognized in the late
nineteenth century as allowing for greater development
of theme and character than a short story without being
burdened with the demands of a full-length novel.

Our broad goal in assembling the Oxford Novellas,
a unique series combining substance and brevity, is to
present the least studied genre from one of the world's
oldest literary traditions which includes one of the
most sophisticated pre-modern poetic theories. At a

time when news is entertainment and literature has to compete with popular fiction, two criteria have guided our selections: socially relevant themes for readers who might want to know things quite outside their experience and understanding, and literary excellence. Thus, famous names march with writers few people have even heard of.

Having absorbed words from nearly four hundred languages, English is opulently equipped to interpret and express the cultural energy of the regions it once entered as the colonizer's voice. If, to paraphrase Wittgenstein, the limits of our language mark the limits of our world, we hope, from time to time, through this series, to move the borders of literary enjoyment further and ever further. Translation into English brings together the creative potential of different Indian languages, the special understanding of the world each one of those languages has, and consequently, the distinctive way they carry the memories and histories of those who use them.

The art of story-telling and the art of narration mingle to give us a literary mosaic made possible by translators working to move texts originally written in other languages into English. We believe that the translator is not merely an echo or a shadow, a reflection or a crib, but a fresh, strong supporting voice that conveys both the said and the equally vital 'unsaid' parts of the original into the receiving language.

MINI KRISHNAN

Author's Note

As I was going through the translation of *Sheet Sahasik Hemantolok* earlier today in order to write the Author's Note, I got goosebumps. Aparajita, my character of twenty-five years ago, seemed so much like me today. Like her, I have trouble with my eyesight and cannot read beyond the headlines without the help of a magnifying glass. Like her, I have continued to write, nevertheless, due to long practice. I look at the back of my hand, and fail to recognize it as my own; whose hand could this be, I wonder, with bluish veins sticking out? That was exactly what my central character Aparajita felt, when she was seventy, in 1988. When I wrote this book, I was still a young woman. I had enough distance to see the problems of ageing with a kind of neutral empathy. And like her, I can feel the existence of a blind spot in my rear vision today. No matter how carefully I look back, I cannot see it all. For example, I cannot see how I appear in the eyes of others, as an elderly woman. Nor could Aparajita. Now that I am her age, I seem to share most of her feelings and realizations. This was how, twenty-five years ago, I had imagined a sensitive woman to feel about life at seventy.

Aparajita, a well-known writer, has come to live in an old age shelter of her own free will, and is trying to write a novel for a periodical's special number, something very different from what she has written so far. She wants to write about her co-residents in that shelter. And she wants to present them through their own narratives by using their dialects and particular ways of speaking. But she is not sure that she can complete the novel – she is running out of time. When she is diagnosed with terminal cancer, the manager of the old age home comments wryly, 'Everyone here is a terminal case anyway'. Ageing is not a gentle experience.

This novella about growing old, being cast away and lonely, was written sitting at a desk in front of a window facing a dreamlike sight. A green island appeared and disappeared in the distance, and white ships floated by on the blue Pacific Ocean. This was in the summer of 1988, I was teaching at the University of British Columbia, surrounded by lively students and colleagues.

I had been approached by a new Bengali magazine that concentrated on hot stuff – mainly films, fashion, sex, and scandal – to write a short novel for their special annual number. At first, I had thought of turning down their offer, given my limited experience and interest in that genre. But on second thoughts, I decided to accept and use the opportunity to write about people who have no place in such magazines. It would be good for everybody, to make some space for them here.

I wanted to write on ageing as I found myself being steadily surrounded by ageing elders. And it bothered me. Twenty-five years ago ageing was not a hot topic in the Western literary world, and it is still not very common in Indian literature. This book is all about survival and sensibilities, about relationships and adjustment. And adjustment is not the same as compromise. This book is about women – middle-class, urban, Bengali women, from a wide variety of socio-cultural backgrounds, living together in an old age shelter. The shelter is like a melting pot, it teaches its members to recognize the nature of reality, shift gears and adjust to changing situations in life, and to make the best of it. I may not be able to change the world by myself, but the world I create as a writer is within my power. Yet, if I were to write this book today, I would perhaps be a little stricter, perhaps a little less kind.

The novella was printed in the magazine's special annual number in autumn, 1988, but came out as a book only in April 1990. The locale and the characters of the book are as distant as they can be from the desk where it was written. But the story was taking shape in my mind for quite some time, ever since I started visiting an old age home for women in Kolkata. Off and on, in my spare time, I would read out my travel-tales and funny stories to the ladies there. They enjoyed listening to lively stories, and hated spiritual lectures, some confessed. I had been carrying the characters in my head for quite a while. When the book came out, it was dedicated to the residents of the old age homes of Kolkata. That the book recognizes their effort to learn to live differently, and to unlearn a lot of their old beliefs pretty late in their lives, was genuinely appreciated by the residents. They also liked the way the book presents ageing as a maturing process, not as wasting away. 'Like a Kashmiri *jamawar* shawl, this tattered, moth-eaten human life grows more precious with age.'

The original title of the book *Sheet-saahosik Hemantalok* was borrowed from a poem by Jibanananda Das. It meant '*A Winter-defying Autumn World*'. I felt *that* name suited my world of brave, elderly women best. In the English edition, the translator and the publisher decided to make the title simpler. Interestingly, the novel has been translated into several Indian languages, but not one has retained the original title. It has been translated mostly as *The Autumn World* (*Hemantalok*).

In this book there is no narrator, the characters speak for themselves. Each has her own narrative, and the story is revealed through these. I have experimented with several layers of language, using various speech registers to identify different individuals. The speakers' linguistic expressions reveal their different social, educational, and cultural backgrounds to the reader. It is a pity that translations can only go so far and no further. I agree with the translator that it might not be possible for an English translation to recreate that intricate use of the local tongues in this particular text, to express the varied backgrounds and colourful personalities of the characters.

However, here is a careful translation, carefully edited, and I am grateful to the translator, Tutun Mukherjee, and my editor, Mini Krishnan, both very dear friends of mine, for taking this book to a wider readership.

NABANEETA DEV SEN

Translator's Note

Nabaneeta Dev Sen is among the few writers attempting to give voice to a marginalized sector of the society by initiating a discussion of the grossly neglected subject – 'Women and Age' in India. As a seminal contribution to the subject, *Sheet Sahasik Hemantolok: Defying Winter* deserves the wider circulation that English can give. Today, translation is no longer seen as an adjunct of literature, but has become a mode of critical engagement with literature, a process of 'carrying across' or 'mirroring' a text from the source language and culture into the receptor language and culture. A translator can have many strategies to enable the text's movement from one language and culture to another, and be alert regarding the 'perils' involved in undertaking such a movement.

Hence, both 'text knowledge' and 'world knowledge' become important realms to recreate, and the translator must choose strategies to evaluate the amount or the kind of knowledge to be shared with the target readers in terms of her/his familiarity with the cultural terms to unveil the linguistic, social, historical, and cultural traces embedded in different linguistic and cultural webs. The translator must therefore be a reader first, who responds reflexively and analytically to the features or values of the source text. Equally important is to be sensitive to 'what' is read and 'how' it is read. There is neither a magic formula for the translator to mechanically adopt, nor can there be a perfectly transparent or a 'final' translation because each reader-translator must make certain choices regarding the issues to highlight and give greater or lesser emphasis, subconsciously or otherwise, to different kinds of values, characteristics, or impressions. The path is rough and the choices are difficult. The relationship between the text and its translator is dynamic and transformative because each text calls for strategies to be arrived at after attentive engagement with it, which includes the consideration of possible alternatives.

A layered text like *Sheet Sahasik Hemantolok* stretches language to its limits and strains the energy of diction to nuance characterization and develop the discourse.

In the original Bengali text, Dev Sen uses varying speech registers for different characters to distinguish their 'individualism' and 'subjectivity'. The language patterns make apparent the 'generation' to which a person belongs, her nature and personality, education and background, class and social status, as well as her philosophy of life. Dev Sen combines several linguistic styles – elevated literary prose and colloquial Bangla, along with the newly fashionable 'Benglish' or the Bengali-English hybrid used by young people who are more at home with English. The most challenging is the use of raw street slang of Kolkata's red light areas. Since Bengalis are generally more class than caste conscious, rather conservative and normative in their behaviour, manifesting more often than not a bourgeois mentality, the speech rhythms serve as a clever rhetorical device for the author. For instance, the literary and emotive Bengali diction of Aparajita, who is a creative writer with a poetic sensibility and represents the receptive consciousness of the text, is different from that of Salajnayani who is simply scripting her life. The colloquial speech rhythms of Jaya's mother are different from those of other inmates, each of whom reflects her culture and mentality through her expression. Of course, the most fascinating of all (and the translator's agony!) is the coarse, vulgar, amoral, and sexually explicit yet racy style of the intriguing Nistarini who comes from the 'dubious' neighbourhood of Rambagan. Yet the subliminal fissures underlying her expression reveal dimensions of her own character and enrich the text with a version of social history. But totally different from her language is her daughter-in-law's speech which is generously sprinkled with English as she comes from a different background and upbringing. So wide is the gap between them that they seem to be residents of two different planets. The noteworthy fact is that as Nistarini evolves as a person during her stay at the 'Twilight Shelter', her language also changes. She is avid to learn new and more valuable lessons of life after she has crossed the age of sixty. Her language traces the development of the new dimensions of her persona and the changing interests in her life.

Thematically, stylistically, and structurally the text is a remarkable achievement that makes the translator's task very daunting indeed. The intractability of English in the transference of idiomatic 'vernaculars' is a well-debated subject. It serves no purpose to re-visit those arguments here. In this context, the point to be emphasized is the loss that has been incurred in not being able to do full justice to the author's style through translation and carry across all the subtleties of the author's use of language. The skill sets of translation like varying the speech rhythms, retaining culture-specific terms, italicizing transliterated English words present in the original text, glossing, have been put to optimum use. It must, however, be reiterated that the entire play of language and idiomatic expressions of Bangla *bhasha* exemplifying the spirit of the text has been difficult to carry across.

In addition to the aspects of translation explained above, translating a womanist text demands sensitivity to a woman's experience and the realization that women and men do not inhabit an identical world, or at least do not view it identically. Such a sexual or gendered perception as a social construct has implications regarding the way a woman's world is understood and interpreted. Dev Sen's writing demands that sensitivity and attention to the details, specificities, and nuances of language and description, which as Helene Cixous explained as *l'ecriture feminine*, make evident the inexhaustible fluidity of feminine imaginary capable of transcending the univocality, linearity, and the fixity of 'phallic' discourse through excess, circularity, and repetition. Cixous explains that a woman's writing can only keep going, 'without ever inscribing or discerning contours ... [because] ... her language does not contain, it carries; it does not hold back, it makes possible' (1976, p. 878). Two other prominent features of Dev Sen's writing are her ironical tone and style. It hasn't been easy to 'carry across' Dev Sen's irony and almost lapidary touch in handling the emotional quotient of the inmates of 'Twilight Shelter', each with her own social-economic-cultural and domestic histories. The many voices heard in the novella convey their unique worlds of experience and understanding in different speech registers and rhythm which alerts one to the dangers of uniformization and the erasure of differences. Translating *Sheet Sahasik Hemantolok* has been as unique an experience as reading the book itself. Vera Nazarian says, 'The world is shaped by two things – stories told and the memories they leave behind.' *Sheet Sahasik Hemantolok* contributes to the re-shaping of the social perception of gendered experience, and the many voices from it cannot but resound in cultural memory.

TUTUN MUKHERJEE

Work Cited

Cixous, Hélène. 1976. 'The Laugh of the Medusa', trans. Keith Cohen and Paula Cohen, *Signs* 1, no. 4, pp. 875–93.

Introduction

We tell ourselves stories in order to live.
—Joan Didion

Being able to tell stories has often marked the line between life and death, whether for a Scheherazade or for the anonymous women choking with untold tales, because narrating stories makes available a mode for realizing one's communal and historical identity since 'who one claims to be' often gets subliminally woven into one's stories. However, a central and often overlooked feature of these stories is the role women have played as narrators and performers, and the related centrality of female figures within a narrative, especially if such a narrative is told or written by a woman. Since classical times male writers have denigrated women storytellers and writers, often referring scornfully to the image of the 'maundering old woman' telling stories by the fire in order to 'scare the little ones or divert the young ladies or amuse the old', or as Hawthorne infamously said, 'a damned mob of scribbling women'. Thus has evolved the term 'old wives' tale' to disparage certain tales as immoral, false, or superstitious. Christine Nufeld explains that her reference to oral culture as 'debased' is intended to emphasize the fact that women were not associated with the formal methods of composition in primary oral cultures but were aligned with the more informal word of mouth aspect of oral traditions (p. 420). Thus, there was an attempt to ghettoize women in oral culture. Not only was such 'storytelling' associated with the private world of women devalued, women's writing, till very recently, was considered irrelevant to literary aesthetics, which thereby promoted a gendering of the discursive literate spheres. As has been pointed out time and again, whereas a woman who sings is called a singer, who dances is a dancer, who paints is a painter, who cooks is a cook, the one who writes is invariably described as a 'woman writer'! Why should such a qualifier be used at all? Why should the act of writing be thus set apart? According to Nabaneeta Dev Sen, this instance of typical male attitude to female creativity was

'... probably because singing, dancing, cooking appeal to the senses ... but the primary appeal of language is to the mind ... the woman who dances, cooks, sings is [considered] within her rights, but the woman who writes? She is not. She has stepped out of area of senses and has appropriated a male gesture. Her appeal with words is to the mind and not to the senses. The power relationship has reversed ... she commits an act of transgression against the social code, has trespassed into male territory ... (p. 298).

The treasure house of Indian literature is replete with stories of all kinds, of varying taste and tone, from different regions and with different cultural affiliations. But the corpus is in its great majority, like most discourses, masculine. Till the late nineteenth century, stories were written mostly by men and formed a part of and contributed to the prevailing patriarchal normative order. Except for a few rare instances, women did not write; at least, they did not write stories to be read by the general – mostly male – readers. This, however, should not suggest that women were totally voiceless. Actually, they remained unfailingly close to the oral traditions of storytelling and found hidden and subversive ways to exercise their agency even while appearing outwardly to remain within a repressive social grid. Women narrated – until they could write them down – stories which comprise a vast archive of 'subjugated knowledges'.

It is well known that during mid-nineteenth century matters of education and literacy became a major discourse in India in which women's social progress figured as a contentious issue and led to now well-known debates between the altruistic colonizers and the indigenist reformers. When new laws were proposed, the colonial authorities readily supported the limiting parameter envisaged for the education of women which was reconfigured within patriarchal ideologies. Although the dilemma was apparent in the way women began to regard themselves, the discourse on women's emancipation and social change in India was initiated as a result of the social churning of mid- and late-nineteenth century, which led to major reorganization in the related areas of social subjectivities and cultural production. While encouraged by a liberal faction of the society – as for instance the Brahmo view of behaviour and conduct of life and religion – the 'New Woman' or *nabeena* emerged, who scorned conventions and readily adopted Western education, attitude, and style of dressing. The majority of Indian women or *pracheena* remained immured in superstition and social evils like child marriage, polygamy, and the privations of widowhood. But, happily, by the second half of the nineteenth century, more women were getting educated. And gradually, they began to write and give expression to their responses about the changing social conditions, including the demand to expand the scope of women's education. They wrote also to emphasize the need for change in women's condition and philosophy of life. Given the times when they lived and the forces they had to counter, the questioning of customs, conventions, and values was of considerable significance. Mandakranta Bose writes, 'Subjected to a multitude of forces, often contradictory, the women of India – not unlike women elsewhere – began to move toward self-perception, self-expression, and self-determination, slowly, indeed, and against tradition' (p. 215). Extremely significant to this gradual evolution was the availability of the print medium. The spread of printing revolutionized the nature and kind of knowledge and information that could be disseminated, which in turn affected the patterns of their circulation and the consumption of texts. This was of particular importance for women because printing provided access to the public sphere hitherto denied to them. As explained by Partha Chatterjee in his book *Nation and Its Fragments*, the encounter of nationalism with Western modernism had initially widened the schism between the private and the public spheres. The general idea was that women inhabiting the private sphere were to be the carriers of tradition and spirituality. But soon, articulate women led literacy drives to stress a modern outlook and women's social emancipation. Bharati Ray clarifies in her insightful survey of the subject that though there weren't radical changes or shifts in the perception of women's role in the family and society, one could, however, trace 'the evolution, albeit slow, of new beliefs shaping their goal, attitude, activities. What began to emerge, although in an embryonic form, were an awareness of and an attempt to change women's subordination and disadvantages under patriarchy' (p. 4). So, until 'education' and 'book learning' were seen to be non-threatening to the traditional role of women, they remained unwelcome and scorned for producing the nabeena/new woman with her Western dress, shoes and cosmetics, defiance of tradition, her novel-and-poetry-reading – a 'blue-stockings' figure caricatured in the literature of the time.

However, the spirit of social critique and reform gradually gathered momentum with the founding of several women's journals and magazines in the late nineteenth and early twentieth centuries. The awakening of women to their rights and 'voice' was helped by the increasing number of women writers who generated wide-ranging discussions on different aspects of women's life and experiences. This was of immense significance as it encouraged education of women, their desire for more independence, and participation in activities outside the home. In her Foreword to a collection of essays by early Bengali women, Tanika Sarkar writes, 'Around the middle of the nineteenth century, a social category was born in Bengal, along with the new word that named it: *lekhika* or the female author. Earlier, women's literary compositions had been predominantly oral, eponymous or anonymous, and fragmentary' (Sarkar 2005, p. ix). Thus the print media enabled women to share their thoughts on a range of issues – from apparel and footwear, to marriage, childbirth, and divorce, to education, culture, and travel. These articulations made evident an emergent binary which distinguished the pracheena or the traditional woman unwilling to step out of the confines imposed by patriarchy from the nabeena or the new woman venturing into the world with new-found confidence. Once begun, the women sought through the articulation of their introspection and response to the socio-cultural milieu, to move beyond the domestic sphere and find place and attention in the public domain.

In Bengal, which had been in the forefront of the 'education for women' movement, education became acceptable for the new *bhadra mahila* (gentlewomen) when it became evident that it would not alter her role at home and would actually inculcate social discipline into her housewifely duties and impose orderliness, economy, and hygiene. According to Malavika Karlekar's well researched study of the early personal narratives of Bengali women, the general curriculum for home education or *antahpur shiksha* contained the usual exhortatory and normative tracts and women's access to learning was in most cases the result of 'sustained efforts by men to make them literate' (Karlekar 1993, p. 10). Yet, the strong desire of women to explore, describe, and share their experiences and find meaning in their lives could not remain stifled for long. Those who wrote were not many in number [estimated 400 works between 1856 and 1910 (ibid., p. 11)] and belonged to the privileged upper class/caste or the *bhadra* samaj [with the significant exception of the actor/courtesan Binodini Dasi. As a colonial hangover, the creative outpouring of the women performers of ritualistic or folk forms, hailing from the lower classes, were not considered cultured or refined enough for serious attention]. Women's appropriation of the new mode of articulation marked a historical moment of freedoms of several kinds – from containment within oral and anonymous expressive modes, from forced silence within the domestic space, and from the oppression of customs and superstitions. The self-confidence with which women started to write ensured, despite many difficulties, the spread of women's literacy and social upliftment. Though many of the early women writers belonged to liberal and Brahmo families like Bamasundari Devi, Saratkumari Chaudhurani, Swarnakumari Devi and her two daughters Hironmoyee Devi and Sarala Devi, Hemantakumari Choudhuri, Prasannamoyee Devi and her daughter Priyambada, Kumudini Mitra; there were also housewives from conservative homes like Kailashbashini Devi, Girindramohini Dasi, and Krishbhabini Dasi and Muslim women like Begum Rokeya Sakhawat Hossain and the lesser-known Khairunnissa Khatun, who wrote what they saw, heard, and felt about life as women and critically debated issues as varied as removal of superstitions, subjugation of women, modern age and modern women, man-woman relationship and customs of marriage, women's dress and footwear, patriotism, communal amity, and so on. The noteworthy fact is that the first autobiography to be written – *Amar Jibon* [My Life] – was by Rassundari Devi who was entirely and secretively self-taught. Having once breached the public-private divide, the women began to write poetry, fiction, essays, even plays. Tanika Sarkar emphasizes the 'transgressive' and 'subversive' pleasure that reading and writing made available to them and hence '… women ardently embraced the book and nurtured for it an illicit passion' (Sarkar 2005, p. x).

Of great significance at this time was the appearance of journals and little magazines which provided a forum for women to write about topical issues for quick dissemination. Swarnakumari Devi and Mokhhodayini Mukhopadhyay also edited journals like *Bharati*, *Banga Mahila*, and *Bamabodhini Patrika* which highlighted the pressing socio-economic issues relating to women. The range of subject matter, style, and treatment of the writings varied, but the concerns were the same – all dealt with women's living conditions, their secret aspirations, and the search for their selfhood. Confined within the *antahpur* (inner courtyard) that defined their lives, they reflected upon social inequalities, gender relations in a stratified society, women's duties, their subjugation and abject dependence on the menfolk. Evidently, the '*bhadra mahila* were under-privileged vis-à-vis the *bhadra lok* [gentlemen]' (Karlekar 2005, p. 9). Life perceived from their vantage point revealed the subliminal layers of experience and new insights which women expressed with frankness and passion. Bengali women began to discover their own reserves of strength through their writing. They explored their relationship with the society and finally prepared to cross the threshold of the antahpur and step out into the world, as it were. This momentous act has been represented with deservedly dialectical magnitude by Rabindranath

Tagore in his novel *Ghare Baire* (1916) [*The Home and the World*, 1919]. Bimala, the female protagonist in Tagore's novel, is escorted by her husband through the long passage that separates the inner quarters of the home from the outer, into the *baithak khana* [sitting room for men] – which, for her, is an unfamiliar and fascinating space with enticing but dangerous charms. Naïve Bimala seems to symbolize India, poised to step into the world of complex politics, as the country's struggle for freedom turned in a decisive direction towards nationhood. In the 1960s, Ashapurna Debi, one of the foremothers of women's self-conscious and reflexive articulations, composed her magnum opus in the form of a trilogy, structured in the mother-daughter continuity-disruption pattern, recording 'through the eyes of strong sensitive women the changing socio-cultural scenes of Bengal through three generations' (Dev Sen 1997, p. vii). The second volume contextualizes the time brilliantly. The eponymous protagonist Subarnalata wants to read and write; she wants to see the world; she wants to be like the liberal 'new woman' (nabeena) of the Brahmo Samaj; she wants to escape the petty games of domination played by her husband and mother-in-law. She wants a room of her own with a balcony which would be her window to the world. Dreaming of education and open skies for herself and her daughters, Subarnalata fights all her life, first with her husband, his conservative family, and the oppressive living conditions of their home, and then with her sons and daughters, who can't understand why their mother can't live a contented life like other women with her comfortable lifestyle and the prevailing social norms. Introducing the novel, Ashapurna writes,

> ... *Subarnalata* is a life story but that is not all. *Subarnalata* is the story of a particular time, a time that has passed but whose shadow still hovers over our social system. *Subarnalata* symbolizes the helpless cry of an imprisoned soul ... sociologists write down the history of a changing society, I have merely tried to draw a curve to depict the change ... (cited by Dev Sen 1997, p. vii).

Women's writing in Bengal grew from strength to strength in the twentieth century and claimed a place in the literary canon. The aspects of life that the feminine imagination embodied, made space for countervailing narratives of recapitulation and enabled the construction of the subjectivities of women. Though energized by the feminist ideology of the West, the women of Bengal fought their own battles to claim agency to articulate their own stories. There was no genre that the women did not choose to write in, representing the political and social upheavals in the nation, region, and community [like the Partition, Independence, 1942 Famine, Tebhaga Movement, Naxal Movement, etc.] – but perhaps the socio-cultural conditions and the economic reasons that had made the domestic fiction of America and England immensely popular with both the authors and the readers, prevailed in the Indian situation too to make narratives, both fictional and personal, the favourite mode of writing for women. Women narrated stories about life – of happiness and suffering, pain, and death – that they had held back for centuries. They wrote them down for others to know … and perhaps, understand.

As writer Vera Nazarian says,

> All stories have a curious and even dangerous power. They are manifestations of truth – yours and mine. And truth is all at once the most wonderful yet terrifying thing in the world, which makes it nearly impossible to handle. It is such a great responsibility that it is best not to tell a story at all unless you know you can do it right. You must be very careful, or without knowing it you can change the world (p. 174).

The act of storytelling also operates as a healing process by giving voice to the lost, the silent, and the suppressed. Telling or listening to stories may not heal a broken bone or soothe a cough but it does hold the power to heal the spirit, strengthen and empower the human mind.

Stories go on, stories endure. Such are the narratives of the women populating Nabaneeta Dev Sen's brilliant novella *Defying Winter* (*Sheet Sahasik Hemantolok* in Bengali, literally, 'A Winter-defying Autumn World'). The novella conveys the spirited raging against 'the dying of the light'. It is a story about ageing which encapsulates a variety of fictionalized experiences and knowledge of the inmates of an old age home. At a time when they long for stability, older people are often called on to face drastic, and sometimes unwelcome, changes – moving home, retirement from a job, and/or the loss of a partner. As their physical powers wane, they are often forced to cope with illness, pain, or loss of mobility. Loneliness is a very real problem, as contemporaries die and families move. They become increasingly aware that their life on earth is nearly over and many are afraid of dying. The ultimate penalty of ageing for many is when in the mechanical sense the biological metabolism begins to break down and individuals are infantilized by their own bodies. Hence, it is not surprising that when people are culturally conditioned to be dependent and helpless past a certain age; they are more likely to become so, with sad consequences for their own lives and those of others. Consequently, old age is regarded with intolerance, disrespect, and neglect.

Dev Sen's lifelong engagement with women-centred studies has sensitized her to the need to focus upon this still severely neglected subject of ageing women. The 'Twilight Shelter' in *Defying Winter*, or the home for the aged is an example of proliferating 'shelters' for the aged in various metropolises and suburbs have come to serve as alternatives to 'Vrindavan-Mathura-Kashi' as the *vanaprastha* destination of the lonely and/or destitute and abandoned older women of our modern societies. Dev Sen's discourse of age presents the negotiations of selfhood through the experience of ageing. 'Twilight Shelter' presents a social microcosm inhabited by women coming from a variety of backgrounds and situations and each inmate is individualized. Every stereotypical image is demolished and each personality is sharply etched as every one of them fights her separate battle of life. What Dev Sen does not allow them to do is to 'Go gently into that good night', but maintain the mood of the speaker of Dylan Thomas' memorable poem: 'burn and rave at close of day/Rage, rage against the dying of the light.' 'Twilight Shelter' presents a cross section of the society. Persons from different economic and social backgrounds have to learn to live together. The stories of 'Twilight Shelter' show that living in close proximity can create different sorts of tensions among the members; it can also encourage deep bonds of understanding and compassion. The novella is structured as a series of cross-cutting monologues that provide insight into the character of the speaker as well as provide essential details about the other inmates of the shelter: describing their helplessness, anxieties, and compulsions. The novella opens with Aparajita's story. Her's is the framing narrative and serves as a mirror to the others and becomes the thread that links their individual memoirs. She is a creative writer who has gained success and security through her writing. At the close of her life, she decides to leave her home in a desperate effort to buy peace from her insensitive and selfish daughter-in-law Jaya. Aparajita means 'the unvanquished'. Undeterred by age, loneliness, or terminal disease, Aparajita battles for dignity and self-respect. She does not surrender to pressures of age but retains her self reliance. She earns her keep through her creative writing and, actually, the house that she leaves for her son and daughter-in-law has been built with her earnings. The second voice is that of Jaya's mother. She is a simple woman who feels embarrassed that she should live in a house that denied shelter to Aparajita in her old age. In fact, every inmate of the old age home has a poignant story to tell; each has a separate reason for living at the shelter. There are Salajnayani and Binapani; Chiki and Vandana and Romola; and there is the inimical Nistarini. All are 'compelled' by some reason or the other to seek the lonely comfort of the 'Twilight Shelter'. Each character also makes apparent the variety of circumstances and experiences the Indian woman must face in search of peace and privacy in life. Each character tells her story. Their various narratives refract the similar yet subtle difference of each life like that of Protima or Zulekha or Mrs Biswas. Away from the typical domestic sphere, their lives at the shelter expand in dimensions and acquire new meaning. Their lives interweave at the shelter and often lead to rare and precious bonding among them. New kinds of understanding and appreciation of life unfold. The narratives also make apparent both the self-centredness and selflessness of the old. The spirit of the *Defying Winter* is reflected in the following poem by Dev Sen:

Stay alive
Show yourself clearly
Like an unfading passport photo
Stay awake in every line, you,
Like and unquenchable thirst,
Yes you,
The pain that tears my heart apart
Show yourself clearly
Like a flower in full bloom
Don't hide from me
As long as I live in poetry.

TUTUN MUKHERJEE

Works cited

Bose, Mandakranta (ed.). *Faces of the Feminine in Ancient, Medieval, and Modern India*. New Delhi: Oxford University Press, 2000.

Dev Sen, Nabaneeta. 'Introduction,' *Ashapurna Debi: Subaranalata*, tr. by Gopa Majumdar. New Delhi: Macmillan, 1997.

Didion, Joan. *We Tell Ourselves Stories in Order to Live: Collected Nonfiction*. New York: Knopf Doubleday Publishing Group, 2006.

Karlekar, Malavika. *Voices from Within: Early Personal Narratives of Bengali Women*. Delhi: Oxford University Press, 1993.

Nufeld, Christine. 'Speakerly Women and Scribal Men,' *Oral Traditions*. 14(2) 1999: 420–9.

Ray, Bharati. 'Women of Bengal: Transformation in Ideas and Ideal: 1900–1947', *Social Scientist*. Vol 19. No. 5/6 [May–June, 1991]: 3–23.

Sarkar, Tanik a. 'Introduction', in Malini Bhattacharya and Abhijit Sen (eds), *Talking of Power*. Kolkata: Stree, 2005.

Nazarian, Vera. *Dreams of the Compass Rose*. UK: Wildside Press, 2002.

Aparajita's Narrative

As

if I am standing upon a mountain peak.

From this height up here, I can see paddy fields, rivers, villages, railway tracks, forests, and meadows. I can see human efforts and disappointments. Man's greed and penury, man's nobility. And I can see the sad and colourful path of human love.

I can see everything from the point where I have reached. In fact, I can see almost the whole of life. I have heard that while driving a car, despite the rear-view mirror, the driver always has a blind spot, since the view immediately behind him is not reflected in the mirror. Blind spot – where sight cannot reach. We are never able to see what lies directly behind us. To reach where I stand now, I have had to climb uphill – stepping upon the heaps of accumulated years gathered under my feet – here too lies a blind spot. While it is true that I can see the distant past clearly, yet I can never visualize what I look like from the back, how I appear in the eyes of others, at this point of time. However, I had not realized earlier that age could see so far. I have cataracts in my eyes and my sight is getting hazy. My reading is blurred. Soon, my writing too will come to an end. I am unable to read beyond the headlines of the newspaper without a magnifying lens. I continue to write from habit. But my inner eye has grown more expansive, more far-reaching: becoming clearer, more and more precise, reaching further out every moment. Seated in this chair, I can perceive the threefold panorama of Time – past, present, and future – unfold before my eyes. Could I have experienced it before? No. Can my son and his wife do so? They can't. It is not their fault. I couldn't see either, at their age. My inner eye had not opened then. I was blind. Blind? People may call me sightless now; they can say that my vision is dim, eyes cataract-filmed; yet I know that it is now that I have really learned to see. At last, after all this time I have finally acquired vision.

I had no idea what 'vision' meant, till now. Merely the trivial, the ordinary, the apparent, only the unimportant, the dying and the passing had kept me occupied through the years. Just as my son and his wife are now engrossed. Alas. Youth! Youth and its intoxication! Its sudden, heady arrival overpowering childhood and adolescence, devastates everything, creates havoc. It's the body's victory over the mind. The power of physical passion sweeps away year after year. The silent arrival of middle age is barely noticed. When middle age has settled in and the footsteps of old age are heard, then we are shaken out of our *dreams* with the realization that youth was long gone! Youth arrives with a lot of fanfare, like a king, it leaves surreptitiously, like a thief. Yes, a thief. Everything is surrendered to it. Youth lays claim and takes it all. Then, breaking trust, it bundles up its booty and vanishes forever. Noiselessly. With hardly a warning. A couple of grey hairs, a wrinkle or two, a slight breathlessness on the last two steps of the stairs, one or two missed trams, or buses that moved too fast – just those are its signs of farewell, waving goodbye, whatever you may call it.

I am a woman; at least I know that certain parts of my body signal the arrival and the departure of youth, in the manner of the unlocking and the locking up of a door. Men have no way of knowing even that. They feel only the arrival of youth and not its departure. But that is not how it is. For them too, there is a farewell for sure. But no awareness. That's why men continue to be fooled throughout their lives. They think that their youth is eternal while women's youth is transient. To flaunt youthfulness forever and indulge in a lifelong play of passion is a man's prerogative. Women are the commodities, never the consumers. The consumers do not consider their own qualities. They judge the merit of the commodity.

Every creation anticipates its end. Only humankind seems to be oblivious of this fact. 'Day by day we race towards the end, yet we remain blissfully unaware of death – this is the most amazing fact of life' was Yuddhishthir's answer to Dharma when he came to test him in the guise of a crane. The meaning of that statement is clear to me now.

As a child, I had read that 'the puppet has eyes but cannot see; it has ears but cannot hear; possesses hands and feet, but …' meaning that in spite of its eyes, ears, and limbs the puppet has nothing. It isn't human.

But did I know that the irony of Time transfigures human beings into puppets? Gradually, Time robs eyes of sight, ears of hearing, tongue of taste, and skin of the pleasures of touch. The human being becomes a puppet. Even the keenest mind, the most alert consciousness is unable to stop the inevitable seizure.

But the loss of the senses teaches us one significant lesson: that of waiting. I am learning that lesson now.

[*Note:* The words and sentences printed in italics in narratives such as Chiki's, Binapani's, and Romola's indicate the transliterated English words and sentences used in the original text.]

The Mother-in-law's Narrative

What can I call this if not a scandal? Embarrassingly, I find myself in the middle of it all.

The fault is entirely Jaya's. *Beyan* too ignored my requests. I mustn't blame her just because she happens to be Jaya's mother-in-law. She truly tried to do her best. That the house is in her name is not her fault. After all, it was built with her own savings. But Jaya made an issue of it every minute and her barbed comments never stopped. 'You got the house registered in your name. Why, would your son have stopped you from living here?' 'Really, you are kindness incarnate! So generous of you, to offer us a roof over our heads.' 'Very alert, isn't she, about matters of property? Yet pretends as though she is above such trifles, lost in sublime thoughts.... ' These were the kind of malicious remarks Jaya directed at her constantly. How long could she bear it? She finally transferred the property to her son and removed herself from the scene. Just to please Jaya. But the house wasn't registered in Jaya's name, so how would Jaya be pleased? It's very difficult to make Jaya happy, I know it, and now my son-in-law knows. Jaya immediately brought me over, she's not keeping too well, who'll look after Gablu? So I had to come, but I find no comfort in being here. Its like, 'Their riches are not theirs any more, the outsider laps up the cream.'

The more I observe Jaya, the more shattered I get. She seems to have inherited, in full, her father's domineering nature. Who knows, after twenty years, even her husband may be forced like his mother, to transfer the house to Jaya and leave for the 'Twilight Shelter'! Look at the way Jaya treats her own mother! Doesn't her husband notice all this?

But Beyan seems quite content at the 'Twilight Shelter'. As if that's been her home forever. When we visit her, she is happy; when we don't, she doesn't appear sad. But watching her, I am getting ripened, and well boiled, inside. Beyan is a fine person, but it's not easy to understand her.

'They'll say that Romu took everything and threw his mother out of her home. Please, mother, don't humiliate me in front of others like this. I won't be able to show my face....' When Ramen pleaded with her, she replied with a smile, 'Just don't tell anyone that the house has been transferred to you. And really,

I'm leaving of my own accord – you tell the others, "it was impossible to make her stay. She left because she found it difficult to write here"'. Well, if not her son, her daughter-in-law certainly broadcast that, exaggerating it tenfold. And could Jaya refrain from announcing the matter of the property transfer? She telephoned people and complained, 'She found it difficult to write here, so she shoved the house on us and escaped. We're left to shoulder the phone bills, the current bills, the municipal taxes – he's also lost his house rent allowance in the bargain – just imagine her hostility! Now free of all hassles, the mother-in-law sits comfortably on the breezy seventh floor, being served timely lunches and timely dinners, and writing to her heart's content! And here, we are …' There was no plugging Jaya's mouth. While she lived here, the ma-in-law caused Jaya immense discomfort; and after she's left, she is still giving her no peace. The sharp pain that forces the mistress of a house to abandon her own home voluntarily – won't Jaya get a taste of that herself some day? I wonder! Gablu too will bring home a bride one day. Doesn't Jaya think of that?

But it's truly difficult to understand Beyan. You know, after her widowhood she had stopped eating fish or flesh. Yet, after twenty-two years, when my husband died, she ate fish for my sake, just to give me the moral courage, she kept me company. What a remarkable person she is. Jaya hadn't spared her even for that. But she never reacted to Jaya's poisoned remarks, as though Jaya was her mother-in-law and she the daughter-in-law. She would silently leave the room. Perhaps the barbs had pierced her finally, and she had found Jaya's tongue unbearable. Who'll guess from the kind of language she uses that Jaya had an MSc degree? What can I say, she's my daughter after all. But she's not in the least like me and has taken wholly after her father. Both in her looks and her behaviour. My son-in-law is a sheep in front of his beautiful wife. How could he allow his old mother to leave? I still can't fathom it, no matter what his wife might have said! Jaya has beauty, infinite energy, and a sharp tongue. Why won't the man be under her thumb?

Jaya has an unbelievable aptitude for hard work and harsh speech. Her husband has a soft, amicable nature – a peace-loving creature. Jaya doesn't spare him at all. Night and day she nags, 'A timid egg! That's what you are. You can neither speak up for your rights at the office nor scold the servants at home. You can't even discipline your own child!'

Timid he certainly is. Otherwise, can one be so afraid of one's wife as to snatch away the shelter from one's old mother and turn her out of her own home?

My son-in-law is a mild-mannered, peace-loving man, willing to do anything to avoid trouble. Even if it is a morally wrong thing to do. That's his given nature. A very weak man. Just the opposite of Jaya. Jaya is domineering like her father and extremely quarrelsome. Her husband doesn't dare to argue with her. On top of that, my daughter is beautiful. Men surrender helplessly to beauty. Gablu misses his grandmother and cries for her; Jaya scolds him. Gablu's sobs can be heard. Those of his father's – Jaya can't hear; but I can. He sits down at mealtime, unmindfully fingers the food on his plate, and gets up. I can understand. His mother always sat by him, supervising his meals when he ate. It wrings my heart. But who am I? I'm an outsider. He calls me 'mother' too, but can a mother-in-law ever be the mother?

Jaya's expecting a baby, I have to be here. But won't people accuse me? They'll say that I've sent Jaya's mother-in-law away to come and stay here myself. But, I sincerely want her to return home. I live in Beyan's house while she stays away in a boarding house in the very same city. What a peculiar arrangement! I feel embarassed even to show my face on the balcony.

I think Jaya is envious of her mother-in-law. Perhaps Jaya feels small in the face of Beyan's social prestige and economic independence. In spite of her beauty, her MSc degree, her husband's riches, Jaya doesn't have what her mother-in-law has, the divine blessing of creativity. Can everybody possess that?

God bestows his gifts where he pleases. I can't make Jaya understand because she doesn't listen to me. I'm just a matriculate and have never attended college; she doesn't regard me as a complete human being. She's her father's daughter and will always be like him. Her father had never tried to understand me; nor does Jaya. They do not try to understand anybody, ever.... She didn't understand Beyan.

Jaya seems quite cheerful now. She does not understand her husband either. His face seems to have lost its glow. Jaya attends cookery classes these days and tries out new recipes now and then. This is her fifth month running, she has recovered her normal health. But these new dishes almost bring tears to my eyes. Doesn't she have any feelings at all? I wonder what terrible stuff poor Beyan gets to eat at the boarding house. Is it easy to relocate yourself at this age?

Aparajita's Narrative

Why not try a different kind of novel for the Puja Special this year? I am tired of writing the same kind of stuff for so many years – and I can't say I have written very little in my sixty-seven years! Your eyes must be tired of reading the same stuff too. But all that bloody nonsense was lapped up by you! Language? Yes, my language is becoming a bit raw. Agreed. But all of this is not exactly my language; it is Nistarini's. Nistarini, Salajnayani, Binapanidi, Chiki, Romola, Geeta, Vandana – they are all here. Their idiom and style of speech merge into mine sometimes.

It is no longer simple to remember things separately at this stage and maintain the subtle differences. Besides, it isn't easy to make Nistarini and Romola, Romola and Salajnayani, mingle together. At least, let me start the novel, though I am not sure whether it will be finished. I have been diagnosed with a terminal disease after I came here. If the end comes abruptly, let it. But I insisted on coming back here from the hospital. That was my wish. No, I do not want chemotherapy. I shall write as long I'm able to move my fingers. I am writing three novels at once. I shall experiment with other ideas in those two; this one will be different. The doctor has given me a maximum of three years. That's a lot of time. I have started homeopathy. There is no pain yet. The homeopathy doctor told me that he can't defer death, but he can defer pain. I shall continue my work as long as it is possible, as long as there is no pain. Let's see! Home? No! What's the point in going home?

This is better. My room is so pleasant here, restful. I've written nearly a hundred and fifty books from home. Those books provided me a house to live in and a car in this city. When I vacated the rented house, the house-owner's son was delighted. One doesn't do such things these days. The landlords used to get three hundred earlier; now they are getting three thousand. Now, 'returning home' means not going back to my familiar rented flat, but going back to live with my son and daughter-in-law.

I know everybody thinks that the last days of life must be spent with one's near and dear ones. So, why have I returned to the 'Twilight Shelter' instead of going home? My disease was diagnosed after I came here. Would they be willing to take me back or not was my main worry. Would anybody willingly accept a terminal cancer patient? But they did. The secretary, Dhrubajyoti Babu is an interesting man. He said, 'Terminal case? So what? All are terminal cases here! It is our good fortune that you chose to live with us. You are most welcome, indeed, since the costs of your treatment are your own!' Dhrubajyoti himself is about sixty. He is trying to turn this place into a shelter for both men and women. But I'm trying to make this novel a story excluding men. What's the harm? Why shouldn't there be man-less novels? We know real life is neither a play nor a novel and useless words like man-less or woman-less have no meaning in life. Those words belong to the world of literature, coined to suit our convenience. But novels? I often wonder if one could write a novel depicting life exactly as it is, would that make a good novel? No, it wouldn't. No one would read it.

No one would read it not because it lacked excitement but because it just wouldn't seem credible. No wonder Shakespeare had remarked, 'There are such things in heaven and earth, dear Horatio, that are not dreamt of in your philosophy'. Fantastical like fairytales, monstrous like horror stories, funny like cartoons, and unbelievably sweet like romances, are the actual incidents that happen in our life. So much so, that sometimes reality itself appears exaggerated. You will not believe me if I write about such matters. You will not read my novels. You will say, 'Go on, can such things really happen?' Therefore, to make things seem 'real', very often we prune, modify, and twist the truth, and make it appear complex because that is what 'real life' is believed to be.

At the 'Twilight Shelter', life keeps its last lamp burning. There is provision here to replenish the oil, hands are ready to trim the wick, and arrangements are made so that the flame may live forever like the Olympic torch! How can you find any drama here? Drama takes place in the sphere of activity. This is an interval. The final climax of every individual's life is yet to come. Life's drama usually occurs in the life lived outside. In youth. During middle age. In the household. Here, life is lived mostly in the mind. The 'Twilight Shelter' is not a household. It signifies a retreat from life, like *vanaprastha*. Since retiring to a forest is not feasible, in 1988, this new concept of vanaprastha was borrowed from the West. So that when domestic activities cease and people like me start playing the role of extras instead of adding to the crowd at home, they might seek mental and physical rest in retreats such as these. Something like a big umbrella. Nest? No, this isn't the time to set up nests. The name is not very appropriate in that sense. But as Jibanananda said, 'all birds return home, all rivers/the business of life comes to an end. Only darkness remains.' This is that darkness. Each of us has carried in our bosom our precious wild creeper, the *Banalata*. Now is the time to sit face to face with it, night and day. But those who don't possess their Banalata? Not everybody is blessed with a Banalata, you see. Most people are not.

Those who don't have the Banalata in their heart, argue about the size of the fish fillet. Or, the watery taste of the milk. They complain: 'Why does she keep the light on? It disturbs my sleep.' 'Why are the windows left open? I feel cold.' Another is claustrophobic and breathless when the window is shut. If one stops reading, another suffers insomnia!

What can I do about it?

Here, the rooms are of different sizes. To suit the pocket of each person. Just as hotels have rooms of different rates, this too is something like that. And a garden! A very beautiful garden. A lawn covered with green grass open to all. Although the building has seven floors, the entire building is not occupied by the Shelter. Just the five upper floors. Yes, the lift works day and night. There is a generator for power failure. No inconvenience at all.

Some rooms accommodate three, some two, and some have single occupancy. All the rooms on the seventh floor are air-conditioned. Every floor has a different arrangement and rates vary. The meals vary, too. In the floor below ours, we have the library, the music room, and the common room, these are shared by all. There is a game corner too, where we can play cards or chess. Every floor has a separate dining hall and a small lobby, it is provided with a television set. Not bad at all. The arrangements are quite satisfactory. Dhrubajyoti Babu is a hard-working man. The girl who looks after us (her name reflects the melody of our evening years: it is Purabi) is only about twenty-eight or twenty-nine. Life overflows through her, kind maternal care spills into her actions. Dhrubajyoti Babu and Purabi have together managed to induce fresh energy into the lives of the fifty *vanaprasthee* inmates. What will happen to us if Purabi gets married, remains our constant worry. We can't deny possibilities of secretly nursing extremely selfish thoughts in this connection. Old age is supposed to enhance your patience and forbearance, make you more generous and noble, diminish selfishness – well, that is what I used to think once upon a time. Now I can see – I can see that the bitterness of an entire lifetime settles like condensed milk in your old age.

Has that happened to me too? I should have aged much more within over the last sixty-seven years, but I didn't even notice how the years flew! Does everyone feel this way? If not everyone, I am sure many do. I've realized that only after coming here. As I write this novel, I have a sense of guilt, perhaps I am being unfair – towards the past, and towards the future. Yes, the future. Can't I think of the future just because I am here? Is this to be an eternal present, 'every day'? Certainly not. This is not Dante's *Inferno* and the entrance does not carry the notice: 'those who enter here leave your hopes behind', like a pair of slippers! Those of us who come here, come with a lot of hope. But hope of a different kind, different tune, different scale. It may even be called faith. This shelter assures its inmates in a strong voice that old age does not mean the end of everything; it does not mean being rejected as human beings. Old age has its place in the world, it has a distinct role in life. Just as middle age does. Repose is as valuable as labour. We too have our own rights, our claims upon this earth; we have earned those rights at the price of our age. No one has gifted us our space on earth out of kindness. Just as the earth belonged to me during my adolescence and youth, it still belongs to me in my old age. As long as I breathe, and through me flows the air of this planet – so long the earth will be mine!

Youth tries hard to make us forget this. It is in the nature of youth to snatch away things; it says, 'Out! Your time is over, vacate the seat, your ticket has lapsed. The earth is ours now.' We feel like thieves, stealing others' time, in the busy world. But here? It is living in one's own space on one's own terms. 'Twilight Shelter' is no place for youth. Here, we are all elderly, similar in age, all experienced in life. Some of us have understood life; some haven't. Life is shrewd; it doesn't allow everyone to master it easily. But away from the bloodshot gaze of youth, the shrivelled petals bloom again. The life-force that was drying up under the burning willpower of the active world, regains its strength along with recovered self-esteem. Old age is valued here. In how many persons have I noticed the magical transformation from constriction to expansion, within this one single year! The span of life increases here, of that I am sure.

'Twilight Shelter'
One — Sreemayi's Aunt

'Compelled,' declares Binapani Sanyal. Sreemayi darts a quick glance at her Aunt when she hears this. But her Aunt remains unresponsive.

'No one comes here unless compelled. Understand? Would anyone be here if there were an alternative? When your niece is imploring you and is sincerely trying to stop you, then why insist on staying here?' After listening to Binapani's comments, Nirmala pulls the *anchal* of the broad red-bordered sari over her head and quietly leaves the room.

'What's the compulsion?' Binapani speaks again. 'People come here forced by different circumstances. Some have no shelter after retirement; some are childless; some have husbands who are as good as dead. If someone has all her children living abroad, another has run away in fear from her seven sons who want her back. While one doesn't wish to live in the son-in-law's house, the other refuses to live under her daughter-in-law's dispensation; some are forced to flee the strictures of their daughters-in-law while others are left here by their relatives, as though exiled in a forest. The reasons that have brought us here are various and difficult to enumerate. But, look, when you're invited so affectionately then why shouldn't you stay with your niece? There are many here who've never married, have always lived alone and independently on their own earnings, they prefer not to stay with nephews or nieces at their age because they find it difficult to adjust since they're not habituated.'

'It's the same for me,' Aunt interrupts Binapani. 'I'm used to an independent lifestyle – I've been a school-teacher all my life. I retired after thirty-nine years, having joined service when I was only twenty-one or twenty-two. While my mother was alive, I lived with her. There was no problem. Now that Mother's dead, the house belongs to my brother. It's become very inconvenient. Mother died – about three years back. I've tried these three years – but I simply can not adjust.'

Sreemayi says, 'I'm asking *Mejo Pishima* to come with me. Don't stay with my mother or my uncle's wife, I'm asking you to come and stay with me. You have lived with us for a while and you know the way we honour and respect you. Your son-in-law likes you and my son? Have you considered how much Khoka'll miss you? You could give me the money you're willing to pay these people, may be then you'll feel no obligation. It'll be easy for us too. Why must you stay like this among strangers at this age? Shouldn't you at least think of Khoka?'

Aunt stares through the window at the two birds enjoying a dust bath. She does not respond. *Bordi* speaks. She is probably younger than Sreemayi; she has never married. She is the superintendent here. 'Having come, why don't you take an application form? Go home and think it over, if you wish. There is space; no need to hurry. Take your time.'

Bordi has a sweet smile.

'No one comes here unless compelled. We've been forced to come. There was no choice. You have the chance to think it over carefully,' Binapani adds. She wears her sari with an inch-wide border in the smart, modern fashion and her spectacles have thick lenses.

'There's nothing to think over,' Aunt says quietly. 'I've thought this over for a long time. I wanted to come away soon after Mother died. That's when Sreemayi's Khoka was born and Sreemayi came home to her mother. She was recovering after the caesarian. Her own mother was seriously ill too, so I had to stay back, it wasn't possible to leave. Now Sreemayi is well, her mother is well, Khoka is well. So I want my holiday now. Yes, please give me the form.'

Now Sreemayi gets upset. She says, 'Why? Why talk of a holiday, Mejo Pishima? Don't you get time off at home? What's the work that you do? Have you to do anything for Khoka? Isn't Sumitra there to help? Haven't I been there too all these days? I must now get back to my classes – only during the morning though. Keeping an eye on Sumitra, to make sure that she does the work, that's all you need to do. You like playing with Khoka yourself, don't you?

'You needn't worry about how I spend my time. And no matter how much I like Khoka, I feel that I'm being exploited. That I cannot allow. It's a matter of principle – that's all.'

Sreemayi appears quite scandalized. 'Exploitation? Where is the exploitation? How does it break your principles? I truly don't understand any of this. You're there, but I'm there too, and there's Khoka's nanny for twenty-four hours, cleaning and feeding him. You don't have any responsibility. You're not asked to do any housework, Mejo Pishima, not even baby-sitting. Where's the exploitation?'

'Well, I don't know all that. But I can't go to Delhi with you. I want to come and live here. What, are you, or aren't you giving me the form?'

'Why not go to Delhi? Nice place,' Binapani says. 'It'll be very good for the baby too; can a mother's love compare with that of a grandmother's? Your company will be of a different nature ...'

'That's it. That's it. My company is being exploited, and my time. Does my time have no value just because I'm a retired person? Since when have I been begging you? Get me a form, please get me a form, there won't be place left in the end. Did you bring it? Now that I've come here myself, you come along to stop me for selfish reasons. I am not going to Delhi at this age; extreme climate, as cold in winter as it's hot in summer, with dust storms blowing – no, I can't make it, it's not possible for me. Why don't you take your parents along? Your father's retired now. Why me?'

'How can mother and father come with me, leaving their own home and their other grandchildren?'

The Aunt exploded. 'So? Just because I'm alone, just because I'm by myself, you think you can use me? Oh no, you cannot. My time's my own. I shall stay here. I shall stay where I please. When I wish to go to Delhi, I shall. But not to be used by you. She has no work, so make her do something! She has no home, no one to call her own, she is alone, a spinster, she has nothing to do, therefore use her – no way! That will not happen. My time's for my own use. Whatever that may be.'

Sreemayi says nothing more.

Binapani Sanyal is also silent.

Bordi is already holding out the form. Aunt takes it, puts it in her handbag and asks, 'I heard that you've started a non-formal school here, can I teach in that school for free? I've done my teachers' training.'

Sreemayi was waiting in the car. She could hear Bordi saying, 'Isn't it surprising that nearly one-third of the people who come here were school-teachers? Comparatively, few are housewives. Many taught in colleges, many held good jobs – they stay here at their own cost.'

'Some housewives also pay for their stay themselves – but most have no income of their own – their son, daughter, brother-in-law, some relative or the other sends the money. Isn't that so, Bordi?' Binapani looks at Purabi.

'Do they pay regularly? Or are there dues?'

Slightly embarrassed by Aunt's question, Bordi exchanges glances with Binapani and smiles. Both suddenly fall silent. As Sreemayi sounds the horn impatiently, Aunt descends the steps and says, 'I shall bring the deposit next week.'

Aparajita's Narrative

The sun is going down.

A stretch of water lies beyond the trees. More trees beyond the water. Beyond the water, beyond the trees, beyond the rail tracks, is the sunset station. When the day train chugs in there, the sun sets like a good little boy. But at the time of its departure, it turns the water and the sky into a river of blood. But a little before that moment, by the side of that tousled-headed tree there, I paste another sun against that sky. Call it a sun or a moon. I hold both in my hands. Brilliant, light-radiating, translucent sphere. How do I do that? Very simple. Although this room isn't air-conditioned at the moment, the window on that side has fixed panes that cannot be opened. One has merely to switch on the white dome of light swinging from the ceiling. This lighted dome is reflected on the fixed glass pane. A sphere of bright light lolls in the vast emptiness outside, like a pendant. Freed from the confines of the room, it becomes a make-believe sun, a make-believe moon. The curtain should be drawn. But I don't do so. It is so fascinating to watch! Little by little, the pink water turns dark, the sky makes its bed by the side of the water and lies down. Under the net of darkness, water and the sky mingle, till it is no longer possible to tell them apart.

I'm glad I came here. It was a wise decision. At first I was uncertain. Yet I was stubborn, it was the stubbornness of hurt pride. The determination to create an alternative space of my own. Coming here, I've realized that whatever God wills, brings good luck to all. I shouldn't have doubted that. 'Much have you given me, Lord!'

Strange things happen here. The other day when her daughter got married, a boarder's daughter contributed Rs 250 for the inmates to get themselves a treat. That started it! What a quarrel it set off! One said, I want *ilish*, the other said *rabri*; another demanded prawns and yet another, Chinese! Even though the amount was only Rs 250! Incidentally, those who have lived here from the beginning in shared rooms still pay only Rs 250 per month! Many among them have become free boarders, I believe, having lived here for nearly a whole decade. This luxury wing on the sixth and seventh floors was opened just a couple of years ago.

The money for the treat was given to Bordi. How old is Bordi after all? She has come to supervise women of her grandmother's age, while she herself is still under thirty. She has studied sociology for her MA, was enthusiastic about social service, and willingly took up this job. A very nice girl. She takes a lot of care. The minute there is a power cut we see the lower floors lit up brightly on all sides. The generator operates the lights in the hallway, the lift, and the air-conditioned wing. The bathrooms are always swabbed dry by a cleaning woman to ensure that the aged inmates don't slip and fall on a wet floor. She never allows the floors to get slimy. Amazing girl! However, she cannot take a decision about the money. Because the overall picture of old age that one gets here is not an entirely happy one. One assumes that with age, one acquires more patience, more tolerance; that the heart opens up wide like the sky, thoughts flow clean like the all-purifying Ganga; nothing unclean remains. However, this is not the case. I see that some people bring along with them their frog-in-the-well mentality. Till the very last day, they remain prisoners of their own closed minds. I feel really sorry for them.

For instance, what a scene some of the boarders created about Protimadi. Quite shameful. Protimadi was a renowned scholar, a former student of Oxford University, and her books on philosophy continue to be textbooks in the MA syllabus. That a person like her could be treated so miserably, with so much disrespect, I could never have imagined. But the happy thing is, I am not alone here. Many like me are shocked and angry. To loosely generalize that the educated and once-employed boarders are on one side while the 'housewives' are on the other, would be grossly incorrect. No such division exists. In fact, I notice that kindness and generosity are more evident among the housewives. Most of the retired employees seem to share a terrible temper and intolerance. Perhaps they take secret pride in the fact that despite being women in this society, they have earned their living all their lives and are continuing to be independent. Perhaps that clouds their wisdom and judgment. How harmful and how dangerous pride can be, I have learnt this truth after coming here. Those who have nothing to be proud of, take pride in recounting their past. Sometimes that past is just transmitted memory, not what they have seen or experienced themselves, but what was heard in the form of stories from their forefathers. Old age robs us not only of our looks but also of our virtue. It robs one of not just sensitivity but also good sense. Age is a heartless abductor. It does not let one realize when it has quietly bundled away eyesight and hearing along with wisdom and judgement, even kindness, and sympathy. 'Old people should not be told of the death of others of a similar age,' is the general notion. How completely mistaken we are! One cannot know unless one is old oneself. Do very old people get upset at the news of the deaths of other old people?

Not really. The capacity to grieve also diminishes with age. The news of the untimely passing away of younger persons might upset them more, but they are neither anxious nor heartbroken in anticipation when old people are deceased. The 'partially old', those like us, perhaps suffer more. Our group comprises people in the age group of sixty-five to seventy, which is 'partially old', by today's standards. We aren't senile yet. Men don't grow old at sixty/sixty-five. Nor do women, these days.

This Shelter houses only women, and it is precisely that which one calls 'a congregation of all religions'! It shows a wonderful variety of faiths and beliefs. For instance Hindu widows have a choice of meals! One can choose to follow a strict regime and eat only at the vegetarian kitchen. But, if someone wishes to have non-vegetarian meals, she is free to choose it. I appreciate this arrangement from my heart. I have seen many elderly Hindu widows enjoying their fish curry here without any misgivings. It makes me happy to watch them. After all, our life is our own. Every individual has total right over her own body. How can society appropriate that right? Why should our social system be allowed to snatch away colour from our clothes and taste from our food? Just because her husband is dead, should the wife also be pushed out of the periphery of life, deprived of simple human desires? Why must taste, smell, colour be wiped out from her life? The senses are God's gift to all creatures. Why should man deprive her from enjoying that divine blessing?

My mind had always protested against the discriminatory treatment meted out to Hindu widows, though in practice I have devoutly followed the prescribed routine for twenty-two years. From age forty to sixty-two. Then unexpectedly, I changed my practice. That is another story.

My son's father-in-law died suddenly of a stroke when his wife was barely fifty. She, poor thing, gave up eating

fish and meat and stopped wearing colourful clothes.
She was very fond of good food and loved dressing up in
fine clothes. I told her, 'Beyan, this won't do. You must
eat fish. And wear at least light colours.' She said, 'But
you don't, yourself. Why are you telling me?' I knew my
daughter-in-law. I knew that her own mother was afraid
of her. I realized that it wasn't fair of me to make such
demands of another. I said, 'All right, I shall eat fish with
you.' On the day of their *matsyamukhee* rites, I became
a fish-eater after twenty-two years. My daughter-in-law
commented with a smirk, 'If this is what you wanted,
you could have said so earlier.'

Being unaccustomed to the taste for many years, I no
longer relish non-vegetarian food, that's why I don't eat
it. But I am happy to have broken the taboo. It's only
a symbolic act. Actually, I have not really succeeded in
breaking any real barrier in my life. Every time I have
submitted to the tyrannies of tradition. My son too is
the same. Weak. All my high-flying words of rebellion
merely occur in my writing. Now I feel that my work
lacks honesty. As practised by Gandhiji, our life and our
actions must intertwine.

As I was saying, those beyond seventy-seven, seventy-
eight years are not disturbed by the death of the elderly.
Not because they have become calm and *sthitadhee*,
equally unmoved by joy or grief, no! They have enough

interest in worldly matters and are quite alert about their own comforts and sorrows, and get sufficiently agitated over them. One look at the boarders here would make that clear. Yet they show no concern whatsoever about the existence or non-existence of others. But we, the partially old ones, aren't perhaps as prepared for death, and that's why when we hear of the passing away of a contemporary, the heart misses a beat – we wonder is my time drawing near? The thought terrorizes. Knowing full well that the time of departure is close, we desperately desire to hang on to life. Death is utterly unwelcome. I've observed that coming here strengthens our will to live. Here, one does not feel isolated from life, nor lonesome, the sense of being the last and the least disappears, no one is an 'unnecessary burden' here. Everyone is aged, everyone is retired, everyone is seeking rest, and each is alone. They have everything, yet they have nothing in spite of having it all. This is a fantastic state of being. Ha! I too had built my house with a lot of hope, with a whole separate study, just to write in. But …

Here, the newspaper is read out to the elderly inmates every day. Two girls come in and take turns to read to us on alternate days. Earlier, they used to skip reading the obituaries or news items about death. But the television gives all the news anyway; so they have been instructed to read everything. So many have departed this year:

Samar Sen, Manoj Basu, Samaresh Basu, Premendra
Mitra. Perhaps only Samaresh Basu among them hadn't
really reached the time to leave. He went in a hurry,
much too soon. Samar Sen wasn't very old either, but he
had stopped writing. For those of us who did not know
him personally, and had never met him, his presence
or absence did not make a difference. Manoj Basu and
Premendra Mitra had crossed eighty. Not every one at
eighty is like Rabindranath at eighty. The really old did
not appear much disturbed. Our group of sixty-sixty-
five year olds organized condolence meetings for each
of them. We did not know them personally, but were
acquainted with their work. Perhaps the older group will
be saddened by Morarji's demise. India has more or less
accepted Morarji as immortal. He should live to celebrate
his centennary at least. Of what use otherwise would be
all this drinking of his own urine? *Kabiraji* or Ayurvedic,
or Atharva-vedic, who knows which kind of therapy it is?
May Morarji keep well and live long. Each to his own. I
do not care for that kind of longevity, thank you!

Protimadi's matter has been managed beautifully
by that slip of a girl whom everyone calls Bordi. In the
end, they did not submit the written complaint to the
Secretary. They just didn't have the guts to do it. Their
version was that due to extreme senility, Protimadi
had lost her mental balance; she didn't remember

anything, wandered around like a crazy woman with tousled dirty hair, soiled her clothes, and wet her bed. So, she should be evicted. After reading the letter, Bordi, meaning Purabi, smiled sweetly and told them, '"Twilight Shelter" is meant for her, not for people like you. If you are uncomfortable, then you must make alternative arrangements elsewhere. If you wish, you may speak to the Secretary, but he too will tell you the same thing. This Shelter is meant for the disabled, the helpless, the homeless. Actually, if each of you were to contribute only five rupees a month, then she would no longer be the cause of any discomfort. We could arrange a personal attendant for her. At present, there are only seven attendants to care for fifty inmates. It is probably our fault that she is not clean and dry. If we could look after her properly, then such things wouldn't happen.'

No, the boarders did not give five rupees each. But an attendant was appointed by the new arrival – that extraordinary woman who has recently come from Rambagan or Sonagachchi? Her vocabulary is of the gutter, and the unheard-of subject matter of her high-pitched conversations send cold shivers down the spine. It looked like the next general complaint would have been against her. Yet she has voluntarily deposited a whole year's money for keeping an ayah for Protimadi. There is no end to speculations about her. And strange are the stories she joyfully recounts about herself! She has shocked the well-mannered ladies of the shelter into petrified statues. What a woman! A unique wonder! The more I see her, the more amazed I am. Who knew there was still so much to learn, so much to see in life! All this would have remained unknown to me had I not come here.

I am having some problem with this new novel about aging that I have begun. There is no way to keep myself out of it. Shall I increase my age a little? What if I make myself a paralysed patient? Immobility is regarded as the final stage of old age. Isn't it surprising, that no one can tell when the mobility of the mind will cease? You can't see it from the outside. Countless mentally paralysed people walk about in this world. There is no specific age to contract that disease. No time limit.

'Twilight Shelter'
Two – Chiki

– 'Bunty. *This is impossible.*'

– '*Don't be silly*, Chiki. Tutu will return in two weeks – first get the key to the new flat, only then consider the question of quitting. Why be so *impatient? It's not even a year –*'

– 'Had I known what I was getting into – *Tutu has really played a dirty trick on me – too dirty for words ...*'

– 'Chiki, you forget. *Tutu did not propose to you. You did. You do have a short memory,* Chiki.'

– 'Bunty! *I've never heard such language ever before – and what a voice!*

– 'Chiki, Tutu told you about his mother, *I remember quite well.* Tutu told you at the very beginning, mother has a terrible temper, she is *cantankerous* and *moody*, unless you adjust and learn to live with her ... You got into this willingly ...

– 'What willingly? My father is ill-tempered too, but Tutu's mother's *Language* – ? Ugh! *It's straight from the gutter* – you won't really believe it, Bunty, what it's like!'

– 'What won't I believe? That Tutu's mother uses the choicest dirty slang – is that it? Well, the environment determines one's choice of language. What she's heard lifelong is what she's learnt. Your father didn't learn very polished language either during those years in the army. Uncle too uses pretty vulgar words when he is in the army – since it's in English, you don't notice. Doesn't hurt your ears – what sounds extremely *crude* in Bangla, *somehow* doesn't sound so bad in English ...'

– 'Bunty, this conversation is pointless, *irrelevant.* It is not the question of English or Bangla – *she is just incredible in her capacity to be mean. Plain mean and*

dirty, understand? Take yesterday's incident. We were
to go to the Book Fair, hadn't I told her long back? You
arrived and took me in your car – not as though I was
going alone in a bus or something? Or with a boyfriend?
You're my cousin, my own uncle's daughter – not even a
cousin brother. With you – what? Hello? Bunty?'

– 'Go on, go on, I'm listening – I am your own cousin
sister, go on.'

– 'Not a *cocktail* party, or a *play*, or a *movie* – *just* the
Book Fair to buy some books, the *most innocent pleasure*,
in the *open*, in a *public place*. But the crone has such a
dirty *mind*. Do you know what she said? You'll *faint* if
you hear her *choice of words* "going to meet her lover
in the *kunjaban*" and she abused you too, called you
"*Benda sakhi*" or something. She screeches the whole
day, "Tutu has brought this *mlechcha* girl and polluted
my houshold. Her father must be a *kherestan*, sent her to
a *kherestani* school, she walks around in her nightclothes,
drinks tea before brushing her teeth, touches the iron
safe wearing unclean clothes" and on and on and on – I
can't even repeat the *language* she uses, Bunty.'

– 'She still hasn't learnt to *adjust*. Amazing!'

– 'That's the last thing! She – try to *adjust*? Hunh,
that'll be the day! *The most adamant female on earth! She
owns everything, understand? She knows she has power
over every one* – as if we are all her *slaves* in this house.

Others must learn to *adjust* with her, not she. Bunty, *I am quitting – this can't go on – I feel trapped –*'

– 'How are you able to telephone? Isn't someone listening there?'

– 'This is Tutu's phone. There are three connections in this house, you know? All separate connections, one in the crone's room, one is Tutu's, and the third one is in the office. The crone can't overhear even if she picks up her phone – or else she would have certainly spied. *She is so mean, so mean. Look, here – I am quitting*, I'll leave today …'

– 'Why don't you go and spend a few days at Alipur? Why not get out of the house for a bit? You've a car and a driver there – why not go to Alipur every day? Or come to us? Or visit some of your friends? You won't feel so suffocated then.'

– 'Get out a bit? How can I do that? Is the car mine? It's her car, her driver; don't I have to ask her *permission?*'

– 'So ask her. Won't she permit you to visit your father?'

– 'It's better to take a taxi or the mini, than to ask her!'

– 'Don't be stupid. She'll talk rubbish if you take the *public transport* – if you use Buri's car, *she can keep a tab on you*. She must've said those things because you came in our car the other day –'

– 'Yes, if I take the *public transport*, then Buri pours out utter nonsense like "gadding about", "swinging her buttocks on the street", and such horrible things. *In front of all the servants, and there are so many …*'

– 'Better take a maid along, then – that'll be even better –'

– '*Are you crazy*? The *baby* goes to the *park* with an *ayah*! *How about my free will*? Nothing like *freedom* exists in this house *when Tutu isn't here*.'

– 'Be patient a little longer, Chiki? *It'll all work out. Tutu is a sensible boy*. Let him come home –'

– 'He called today. I've told him too.'

– 'Goodness! What did you say?'

– 'I said, *I'm quitting. I've come to the end of my tether. Can't stand her any longer*. I simply can't take it any more … *either I take an overdose of sleeping pills or run away somewhere*.'

– 'What did Tutu say? He's so far away – didn't you think twice before telling him all that? *What can he do from Bombay*? Didn't he scold you properly?'

– 'Why should he scold me? He *coolly* said, *"I suggest you take the latter alternative and run away to Alipur. And stay there*. I'm coming next Wednesday."'

– 'That's what I'm telling you, my dear. Don't even dream of those sleeping pills. Are you mad? *Why should you end your life for that crazy cantankerous female*?'

– 'Going to Alipur and staying there for three days won't solve the *problem*. Won't I have to return? Tutu will again go on tours. *The point of staying here will be lost* if I run away to Alipur every time. Tutu said that *I should try to win her over* – that I cannot do. *Tutu wants me to be with her – just imagine! All the time.*'

– 'In case the old woman is found dead in her lonely room with no one from the family by her side – is that it?'

– '*Not at all.* She has plenty of her own people surrounding her day and night. Kanto's *whole family is dancing attendance on her – and she has her own servants* – that's not the *point*. Actually, Tutu has grown up away from home. Affection grows only from close contact. Who knows how she'll divide the property – that's the worry. *She is quite a whimsical person.*'

– 'And you have all that property! – Married into an old *baniya* family – *half of Kolkata belongs to them –*'

– 'Almost. Do you know how many houses she owns? Thirteen.

Thirteen! Can you imagine? Three huge *mansions*, on Park Street, on Bishop Lefroy Road, and on Theatre Road. All *apartment buildings*. I want to move out of here to the Park Street building – a wonderful flat has fallen vacant. Then there are five houses in the *North* – in Shyambazar, Sovabazar, Hathibagan, and *I can't remember* where else; in Bhawanipur, between Jogubabu's Bazar and Kalighat there are four houses on rent; and on Ballygunj Circular Road, Buri has a beautiful bungalow in a huge garden, *with a lawn, tennis court and what not*! These are only the houses; then there's *cash*, silverware, and jewellery. Just think of that, Bunty.'

– 'Why should I think? That's your job. This is a matter for you to think about. You've already calculated which property she owns where.'

– 'She herself talks about it day and night – *she announces it all day long*!'

– 'Unless you bear with her, why should she give you her property? Ma used to say, *take no pain, win no Krishna*! How many children does she have?'

– 'Tutu's the only son, you know that. There are two sisters – much older.'

– 'That means three *contenders* for the property?'

– 'The sisters are *married*. Even then, sisters too have claims now. Suppose Buri dies without leaving a will? But I don't think that will happen. She understands property matters very well – she must've already made a will; only, *we don't know about it*. Or, she might still make one. That's why Tutu *wants me to be around*.'

– 'Better make sure that the opposite doesn't happen, lets hope that the good is not undone, considering the *sample* of your patience and tolerance that you're showing!'

– 'She loves her daughters. *She's very close to them.* Tutu has mostly stayed away from home for his studies. I fear that they might be given more ...'

– 'So let her give the daughters a few houses. Isn't there enough, Chiki? Suppose your father left everything for Bumba and gave you nothing at all? Would you have liked that?'

– 'Not just the daughters. Aren't the Kantos there too? Suppose she deliberately *deprives* us? That's the reason I can't leave. I know she'll give us nothing the minute we leave. *Buri is quite capable of that sort of thing.* That's why Tutu has warned me, be the housewife *type* here ... *fully domesticated existence*.'

– 'What housewife *type*? Aren't you a housewife? That's what you are! *Not even a working wife.* At least the old woman used to be a *business woman*, you say. For the time being, all you need to do is a bit of cooking, a bit of supervising, care for the home, visit the beauty parlour – dress up – and *what's wrong with that*? No smoking, no drinking, no jeans, no tennis – isn't that all?'

– '*Bab bah*!! There's hell to pay as it is! Smoking, drinking, and tennis on top of that? But I've nothing to do at home. No housework. There are so many servants. Two cooks. One for the old woman, one for us. Two kitchens with two cooks – one non-vegetarian. There're three fridges, one for her, – vegetarian. Another's for us – non-vegetarians. The third one is in the room annexed to the big *baithak khana* outside. It has a sink and a BabyBelling cooking range, its like a small pantry, really. One can store beer and drinks in that fridge, ham-bacon-sausage – everything's *allowed* there. She doesn't mind. *She's rather interesting that way.* Why, she mightn't object even if one cooked *steak* out there! But within the house? My God! *She's a terror.* "This is polluted … that is touched with unclean clothes", she screams the whole day long. There are different servants for dusting, cleaning, mopping, ironing – Buri does nothing in the house herself and doesn't let me do anything either. Two maids do all my work.'

– 'Aren't they there now? Her *spies?*'

– 'No one enters my bedroom without my permission. Nor her room. On her own instructions.'

– '*Interesting.* Doesn't she come herself?'

– '*Never.*'

– 'What does she do the whole day?'

– 'As I said, screams. *She loves to hear her own voice.* She sits for worship for two-three hours in the morning. Before that, she goes for a dip in the Ganga. *Tried to take me too. I flatly refused.* Then I see her cutting vegetables. After that, she's free. Her screams begin from the time she sits down with the vegetables. All day long. Takes a nap in the afternoon. Sometimes watches *video cassettes.*

There's a VCR in her room. She has given us one also. The days she watches the cassettes are the peaceful ones. She likes watching Hindi movies.'

– 'Doesn't she read any books?'

– '*I don't think she can read.* I've never seen her touch a book. Not even the newspaper. But she watches news on the TV. She listens to the share market news from Kanto-da. I think she has some shares – she understands business.'

– '*And yet, she can't read?* What are you saying? Are the eyes gone? She's old after all? May be cataract ...'

– 'Why should the eyes go? She sees very well. She darned Tutu's shawl the other day *like a professional. But she can't be literate.* No educated person can use her kind of language. *She thinks nothing of using four-letter words* – in Bangla – as far as I can follow, all that seems very *evil language* ... I've never heard it before and I can never *repeat* it.'

– 'No! that can't be true'

– 'What do you mean? Why don't you come here one day – *spend a day with me – and you'll know.* What're you doing tomorrow? Tomorrow is Thursday, your college is closed, come over. *It'll be some experience for you.* I tell you, my nature will be spoilt too, if I stay here – I too will become *crude, blunt, and insensitive just like her.* It's difficult to breathe in this environment, Bunty, *it's filthy*

– there's not the slightest refinement – she has no *culture* – but all the property and everything else is in her name. It seems that Tutu's grandfather had left seven houses; his mother added six more – so there are now thirteen – Tutu's father was no good, used to drink night and day, *his liver gave up* – the old woman and Kanto-da's father did all this together, I hear.'

– 'Who's this Kanto-da? Your manager?'

– '*Sort of*. Also the priest. His father was the same, I'm told. Bhattacharjee or something. They've lived in this house for *generations*. Like *family priests*. Looks after the business as well. Funny combination. Buri has paid for Kanto's education. He's passed Costing, Accountancy, and everything. He's kind of nice, though. *Quite cultured*. But very loyal to her. Tutu's not always here, so Kanto-da looks after everything. His wife and children are all here. Buri *is very fond of them*. She depends a lot on Kanto. Tutu's not really an insider in this household, Kanto's like a son to her –'

– 'Then what's the problem? She'll give him everything. You needn't trouble yourself anymore. Chiki. *Relax and leave the place.*'

– 'No, no. Kanto-da's *a nice man.*'

– 'Won't he accept a *gift* because he's a *nice man*? He's not cheating – he's working for it, making her happy – so, he'll get the *baksheesh*.'

– 'Maybe she'll gift him a house – let her – the old woman's a shrewd female. It's not likely that she'll allow the property to go out of the family, but since he's the family priest, maybe she'll give him something.'

– 'Then perhaps she won't give much to the daughters, either. They too are outside the family.'

– 'For them it is a different plan – *she is very very close to her daughters.* They are the offsprings of her youth. Tutu came last. There were five born in between – two between the two daughters and between *Chhordi* and Tutu there were three more. All of them died rather early, *and from various diseases* – I have to listen to these stories day and night – from *pregnancy* to the *funeral! Every detail.* And that's not all. Also about *her love life, her extra-marital affairs, and her business ventures with* Bhattacharjee Moshai.'

– 'What are you saying – *Buri* had *extra-marital affairs?*'

– 'Didn't she? Millions!'

– 'She tells you those stories herself?'

– 'Daily, day and night. *In front of all the servants. She loves to talk about it all.*'

– 'She talks of them herself? To her own son's wife? *Oh, what an amazing woman!* No, I must meet her! I can't wait – must see her with my own two eyes!'

– 'She'll tell you about them too. *She takes a lot of pride in her sexual adventures*. The more enthusiasm she shows in *publicising* those tales, the more *embarrassment* it causes her children. Her daughters have told me repeatedly *not to believe in those stories*. They say that those are the result of her senility, all imaginary tales. She actually had a conservative existence confined within four walls, stuck behind the purdah. The father-in-law used to be away most of the time, rarely coming home, so the mother-in-law made up those horrendous stories to make her husband *jealous*. Now she imagines that those things really happened. *Actually*, none of this had happened. But one can't openly challenge her. That would certainly release a flood of deadly dirty words from her! One must pretend to believe all that she says. *Imagine?* Could our mothers ever talk like that? Well, I don't have my mother, but imagine *Mamima*, your mother? Can you ever imagine her saying such things? Think of that, Bunty?'

– 'Can't she be sent to *an old people's home*, like my mother?'

– '*Are you crazy? This is her house – her estate, her throne as it were*. Why should she leave all this? *What for?* Mamima went because she felt lonely. She wouldn't live with you nor was she able to live alone. That's why she went. But this old woman has a lot of company – Kanto *and his family*.'

– 'I've asked mother a hundred times. But she refused to live in her *jamaibari*, her son-in-law's house. The same *old-fashioned idea. Can't understand her.*'

– 'You call Mamima *old-fashioned? Come and meet Her Highness over here. You'll learn a lot!*'

– 'All right then, Chiki. It shall be tomorrow. *I'm coming over for lunch!*'

'Twilight Shelter'
Three — Salajnayani

Sandhyar Kulaay or the Twilight Shelter.

Yes, the name was chosen by *Kabishekhar* Kalidas Ray. The name for his home. We have borrowed it. Isn't it a nice name? Just what our soul craves for. Just to breathe a little. Isn't that all? But it isn't easy to say, might as well be gone now, not easy to bid goodbye! We have not come here only to depart. We have come to look around. Must go some day. That fact is beyond argument. Since life is governed by mortality, no one in this world can escape the end. No one: not day, not night, not grass, not a flower, not stars, not clouds. Just emptiness remains. Infinite, vast, boundless ocean of emptiness. Yet that emptiness ends too – at the threshold of the planet. Everything ends. Even the ocean. Yes, the ocean is not without bounds. It also has its shore. That's where the ocean ends. That's where the waves crash to death. We in our ignorance mistake the anguish of the dying waves as their gambolling on the beach and become poetically eloquent. What we see is not the playfulness of the waves but the violent throes of their aging bodies. The depth of the ocean ends at the coast. Here it is no longer vast; no longer fathomless; no longer motionless, or profound. The coastline spells the end of all the oceanic qualities. Like it is here for us. We have arrived at our shore here. No matter how desperately we try, no further roads are indicated from here. This is the final point. Waiting for the end.

The coastline advances, the continent advances. The water recedes. It makes space for land as it moves away. Land is of use. It has everything. Everything. Water merely gives birth to the land. As we do. We move away. We willingly make space for youth. Youth is of use. Youth has everything. Happenings. Action. Creation …

There was a big upset at home about my coming to the 'Twilight Shelter'.

My son wouldn't let me come here. He was adamant. 'Listen Ma, no matter how convenient it may be for you, this will mean no end of shame for me. Everyone will say that Babu sent his mother away. They'll say that since it was impossible for you to live with your son, you chose vanaprastha. No Ma, no matter how troublesome it is for you, you must bear with me and stay here. I know that the two of you aren't able to adjust, but should that force you to leave your own home and go away? Just because you have problems with your daughter-in-law? Doesn't your son matter? Should your anger against your daughter-in-law blind you to my social embarrassment?' Despite Babu's anger, I'm convinced that I took the right decision. As long I can move my limbs, hear, and see, I should arrange a private living space for myself where I need not depend on anybody's kindness. Earlier, one went to Kashi or Vrindaban. That's not done any more. Now, there's this 'Twilight Shelter'. What's wrong with it? I'm fine here. Not bad at all. Not staying back at New Alipur in order to protect my son's reputation, has been my wisest move. It is the blessing of Sankataharan Sri Hari, the remover of all perils. My son and daughter-in-law are happy together. I am at peace too. I find a lot of time to read and write. I'm relatively free of social and familial responsibilities here. That wouldn't have been possible at home. Ah, this is the worst curse of a woman's life! Who has harmed whom and how – who said what about whom – who has given or not given what to whom – the inevitable, never-ending circuit of pointless whispering behind one's back – not that this place is free of such gossip sessions. It exists here, too. People behave here just as they do elsewhere in society. Yes, we've lived for a long time – now we are counting our days to the end. Yet we can't change our nature, can we? Such is this incorrigible tendency to gossip. However, people don't drag me into their gossip sessions. They consider me a snob. (She's a writer, you see, so her words and ways, her moods and manners are different! *Aha*, haven't we seen many writers like her before!) Not everybody, though. Romola Chatterjee herself is doubly high-brow. Really, I often wonder why she is here. She has enough money to reign as a queen in a luxury flat with her own ayah, *baburchi*, and *darwan*. She complains all the time – nothing pleases her. Even if I had such financial means, I wouldn't want to live like that! Are you crazy? I wouldn't, because I have lost all interest in household affairs. Because I'm a woman, household duties wouldn't have let me off on their own. So I had to push it all away. But it's different with Renu-di. Where else could she live if not here? She's lost her sight; her hearing too is as good as gone. She has no children. She used to live with her nephew. He's gone away to Canada. Although she can hardly see, she doesn't stop knitting. It's really remarkable. Wherever she might be, whatever she might be doing, talking or watching TV, her hands are always busy. And is she content with that? No, she must involve everyone. She makes them work with crochet, stitch quilts. She's running a little group, Anathbandhu Ashram, 'Friends of the Orphans' at this Shelter! The stuff prepared here are sold at the women's self-help fairs and the money collected is saved in the name of the Anathbandhu Ashram. Sometimes, the money is used to buy books for the children at orphanages, while sometimes in winter, they are gifted the mufflers and the sweaters knitted at the Anathbandhu Ashram. Renu-di has tremendous enthusiasm. She can work hard, too. She says, 'We have just this one life; the more people we can serve, the more fortunate we are. How am I different from the wild animal if I spend this one life all by myself just eating and sleeping?' She is right. I write, and I know the truth of what she says. But Renu-di proves the truth of her statement with her own life, she keeps her word, there is no gap between what she says and what she practises. Renu-di is a true disciple of Gandhiji, her life is her message. But those who indulge in politics these days are not necessarily genuine people. There are countless instances to prove that. The obvious example is that of Shobha-di's MLA brother. Shobha-di cared for and brought up her orphaned brother. She went to work when she was very young while her brother worked for the party. He became an MLA at an early age, but he

isn't so young any more. His wife brought Shobha-di
here. Although people say that she wasn't even sixty
then; she came here when she was only fifty-eight, soon
after her retirement. She'd got a handicap of two years
because of her MLA brother. Perhaps Shobha-di didn't
wish to come here. She keeps to herself, walks in the
garden by herself, and reads in the library by herself. I
have not seen her socialize much.

Our 'Twilight Shelter' is very nicely built. It is a
Varanasi for the aged, after all. It has a meditation room.
There's no separate room for worship since the Shelter
believes in religious harmony. For example, the two
sisters Dolly-di and Lilly-di are Brahmos; so is Renu-di;
and Zulekha-di is a Muslim. They spend a lot of time
in the meditation room. They wouldn't have been
allowed into a room of worship by the sanctimonious
Hindu women, had there been one. That kind is here
too. Nirmala-di performs a ritualistic Lakshmi Puja in
her room every Thursday, Satyanarayan Puja on the full-
moon day, observes Sankranti strictly in accordance with
the Hindu almanac. But for whom does she do all this?
She wears *sindur* in her parting. Her husband has married
a memsahib and resides permanently in London. Her
son lives in New York with his family. Perhaps for their
well-being. The blue foreign envelopes in the name of
Nirmalprabha Bhattacharjee arrive at regular intervals.

So does money. At the time of Puja, a parcel with a white China silk sari material and heavy orlon cardigan is delivered from her son. With the label 'old used'. That, of course, is for the customs. Otherwise the 'duty' to be paid to the post office would be too heavy. This way, it isn't much. Her daughter-in-law carefully washes everything at home. She buys new things and washes them at home before mailing them, to spare Nirmala-di's expenses. Her daughter-in-law had also dragged Nirmala-di twice to America. Nirmala-di couldn't stay there for long. She found it difficult to adjust. She's a devout person. It would have been best for her to have lived in some guru's ashram. She has a single room here. The entire room has been transformed into a puja room. The bed is pushed to one side. Incense, oblation, tulsi plant, lamp, *Ganga jal* – the entire paraphernalia, nothing is missing. The platform with Goddess Lakshmi's seat. Gopal's daily worship. Whoever visits her room can get prasad in the morning – *batasa*, or sugary *elachidana* is distributed every morning. Fruit and sweets are offered every Thursday. Many visit her puja room. Every evening Nirmala-di reads the scriptures – some days she reads the Gita, some days, Bhagavat, and some days, the *Vishnu Purana*. She seems quite content. Those who aren't too keen on TV, arrange their chairs near her room in the evening to listen to Nirmala-di's reading.

But the reading always gets over before the TV serials begin. Nirmala-di herself is quite fond of watching the serials, both Hindi and Bangla. They had lived in Delhi for some time, hence following Hindi isn't a problem for her. But there are many here for whom it is difficult. There are some who are hard of hearing; they manage to grasp some Bangla but can't follow a word of Hindi. But there's hardly anyone here who is illiterate.

Look at Zulekha-di, she has left her husband. Apparently all three wives of her husband are alive and among them, they have eleven children. The family lives in Lahore. She lives alone in Kolkata. She has surrendered her Pakistani citizenship and has returned to her birthplace. She is beautiful – like a ripe mango. It's hard to guess her age. She can't stand Shahabuddin, is a fan of Arif Mohammad Khan, and was shocked and heartbroken when Bangladesh declared itself an Islamic state. She prays loudly for Khomeini's death. At the time of the Shah Bano case, she wrote an agitated letter to *The Statesman* stating: 'Because I am a good Muslim woman, I can't tolerate the beastliness of these fundamentalists. They are not true Muslims. They are harming Islam irreparably.' She had also expressed dissenting sentiments against Rajiv Gandhi regarding the Muslim Women's Divorce Bill. Swinging two snow-white plaits on her shoulders and expressing deep regret

in her *surma*-lined eyes, she had remarked in a sad but
clear voice, that it was extremely unethical on the part
of Jawaharlal's grandson to enforce a Whip to ensure the
passage of the Bill. Zulekha-di speaks flawless English
and Urdu. She is still very beautiful and very careful
about her clothes. A fine French chiffon sari with a lace
border, or a pastel georgette sari, a Japanese silk sari with
a Parsi border, all with a sleeveless blouse. She comes
to our music room sometimes to play the piano, with
velvet slippers on her feet.

Aren't we lucky to have a music room? There
wasn't one before. Binapani-di brought most of these
instruments with her when she came; her esraj, tanpura,
tabla, and harmonium. She brought along her record
player and her collection of records. To these, Nirmala-
di's son added a two-in-one tape deck. From then on,
surprising additions kept arriving in the form of records
and cassettes – gifts received by many from home. All
of us deposited our musical gifts in the music room.
Binapani-di is in-charge of the room. One day, Zulekha-
di brought her piano, and Mrs Biswas her violin.
Everything is kept in this room. It's so convenient to
have a separate music room. Sometimes we organize
soirees here: Rabindrasangeet or Sai bhajan, sometimes
classical music, or a piano or violin recital. We are the
performers. There are many among us who are talented

singers, musicians. Age has not robbed them of their
music. Sometimes professional performers are invited.
Many volunteer and come happily to share their
talent for free with the eager denizens of the 'Twilight
Shelter'. The south-facing music room is Zulekha-di's
favourite retreat. She looks even lovelier when she sits
at the piano, her agile fingers running over the keys,
her pensive eyes gazing at the music sheet. To me, she
looks like a fairy-tale princess, beautiful and mysterious.
It seems that Zulekha-di married several times but had
no children. One of her husbands was an ICS, another
a proper Englishman, an army officer. Zulekha-di is
herself a graduate from Oxford University. Once she
got involved in some scandal with a famous painter
that involved the police and so on. Since she converses
mostly in English, one can count on the fingers of one
hand the number of people she can communicate with.
Most of us find no trouble in reading English; but when
it comes to speaking in the tongue, we're too lazy to
practice. That's why Zulekha-di is friendlier with
Mrs Biswas. They often play the piano and the violin
together. Mrs Biswas is a Christian. She used to teach in
a Catholic school. I wonder why she has chosen to live
here since there are many such 'homes' for Christians.
I've also heard that she grew up in an orphanage. Her
name is Barbara but her language is Bangla. Every

Sunday morning she prays in the meditation room.
A painting of Jesus Christ hangs on the wall by her
bed. That's all. She has a craze for making Christmas
cards. Yes. The whole year she's busy making cards for
Christmas. All of us get cards from her at Christmas
time – beautiful hand-painted ones – and she mails them
to innumerable people all over the globe. She receives
cards in equal numbers, and strings hundreds of cards
across her room like we hang up wet clothes during the
rains. Each day of December and January brings new
cards for her. She was an orphan and had no relatives
but she was once married and had two children. Her
husband has remarried now. She was a working woman
but is a shy person by nature. Everyday she plays her
violin religiously. And Lavanya-di must come to listen
to her everyday. Lavanya-di is the oldest resident of
'Twilight Shelter'. She doesn't like to watch TV. She
walks up with me slowly every evening, leaning on her
walking stick and sits by Mrs Biswas, listening. Who
knows whether Mrs Biswas plays solely for the sake of
Lavanya-di or not? Lavanya-di is now nearly ninety-six
years old. We are planning to celebrate her centenary at
the 'Twilight Shelter' in four years' time. Lavanya-di's
general health isn't bad. Though she appears frail, her
mental and intellectual balance seems to be in good
order, showing no impact of aging. After her cataract

operation, she's able to read too. Her youngest grandson has fitted her with a hearing aid – he too is about to retire. With this aid she can now listen to Mrs Biswas' violin like everybody else. Earlier, she had hearing only in one ear. Lavanya-di is writing a comprehensive book – a cookery book. She dictates and Behula-di writes it down. The first volume has long since gone to the press. The second volume is ready. The third volume is in progress. Lavanya-di has a pink and white complexion, and shoulder length curly white hair. But her head is always covered with a *ghomta* and there is a wrapper around her shoulder, no matter how warm the weather may be. Her spectacles have thick lenses. She always walks with the aid of a stick and with an *ayah* by her side. Her personal ayah. Her grandchildren have made all the arrangements. One pays for her stay, another for the attendant, while a third paid for her operation – Lavanya-di has many grandchildren. They all love her, but Lavanya-di lives here.

Almost all our stories are similar. Everybody loves us, we have everybody, we have everything – yet we are here. Absurd? Why? Why here? Why not at home? Why aren't we in our own homes as the heads of our families? Is it because we are quarrelsome? Is everyone here quarrelsome? Does no one here want peace?

'Twilight Shelter'
Four — Vandana

Rinti would most likely get an engineering seat through the sports quota. Rinti doesn't tell me anything. I lost my husband when I was pregnant. Isn't it only natural for a child who has never known a father to spin his whole world around his mother? He is pushing twenty, and all these years, Rinti has been nurtured by his mother and grandmother. Yet, strangely, he has never been close to me. Instead, he has endless complaints against his mother. While he claims the credit for all his successes, he blames his mother for his failures. For instance, none of the male members of his family, neither his father nor his uncles, had a good head of hair. Rinti too has thin hair. But he blames me for that. Why didn't I perform his *upanayan* during his adolescent years and shave his head to ensure that his hair would grow back thick? Although I assure him repeatedly, 'My dear, I've never shaved my head yet don't I have thick hair? The non-Brahmins never perform the upanayan ceremony, how do they get thick hair? Look around you – you'll find any number of Brahmins who have turned bald in spite of shaving their head for upanayan. Think of that.' But Rinti doesn't listen. He is stubborn like his grandmother. However, there is no love lost between those two. Neither of them can stand me, yet they are not friends. Strange. Rinti is weak in maths; is that my fault too? Yes. Why did I admit him into the Delhi Board? But the good English he's learnt, what of that? The credit for that he claims for himself. He hasn't learnt good Bangla though, despite my getting numerous Bangla books for him, making him write essays, learn verses, recite poems. What more could I do? Still, he hasn't learned Bangla. The fault for that has become mine. The fact that he is not close to me, he now complains, is also my fault. His accusation is that I have always kept him at a distance. Rinti does not acknowledge the fact that at the age of five, his mother had made him learn to play the guitar and taught him to swim. He regards them as his personal achievements! The more I observe him, the more wonderstruck I am. For the last twenty years, my life has been centred around this child of mine. Barely five years after our marriage, my husband died all of a sudden in a train accident, leaving me pregnant with our first child. Only I know how I managed to survive. I could get his job at the office only because fortunately I had a BA Honours degree. Our family wasn't swept away; I stood my ground.

Rinti is an excellent sportsman. He plays cricket. He is a good debater too. He has many admirers. Rinti at least should harbour no complexes about his mother. Yet his lifelong grievance is that he has not received enough attention from me. I'm convinced that his grandmother dinned the idea into his head that his mother was so engrossed in her job that she neglected her child. However, much one tries now, it is impossible to convince him. In fact, it is because of him that I was never able to organize my time well. I was less than twenty-five then. Couldn't I have married again? But I did not. For Rinti's sake. Amit has waited patiently all these years. I have turned him away repeatedly. Only for Rinti's sake. For a son who will never care for his mother. He should forget all his complaints at home after having received so much adulation outside. More than six feet tall, he is really very handsome. He won't escape the trap of girls. No harm in that. As long as he avoids the trap of drugs. He tells me nothing. But I don't think he is into drugs. I wouldn't know, though, even if he was! The world of sports is not a clean one and I've heard that drugging is quite common there. We all know the case of Subhadra Dasgupta, and since then I am scared.

Rinti doesn't lift a finger for the household. A big boy like him could at least buy the vegetables. At home, he acts like a crippled Jagannath. I hear that he works a lot for his college. His father too was a charmer outside and a tyrant at home. His grandmother is the same. Rinti is exactly like her, in his looks and in his nature.

The grandmother has countless complaints against her inauspicious daughter-in-law, who has devoured her son. Yet, she has no one but this widowed daughter-in-law. Her two married daughters live far away. None of them took any responsibility of their mother. One sister paid a visit when her brother died; the other didn't bother to do even that. They make yearly visits to Kolkata to do their shopping and return after the shopping is over. They come bearing gifts of sweets and fruits, and make enquiries about their mother. They take back the news. They don't want to take along their mother. Conversing with their mother means listening to a string of complaints. Like a garland kept ready to hang around the neck of whoever comes asking. The daughters do not like to listen to her unending complaints. They get bored. But there is no option. In Kolkata, they stay with me, in my flat. The daughter-in-law who has been neglecting her mother-in-law because of her career. Doesn't care even for her son. The daughters visit her once a year and stay with me in my flat. They stay a few days, shop, watch movies, spend some time with their mother, listen to her endless list of complaints against their brother's wife, and leave. The two of them have two different type of temperaments. The elder one argues and tries to persuade her mother that actually the daughter-in-law isn't so bad and doesn't really neglect her, and that her own daughter-in-law is far worse. The second one, younger to me and childless, listens silently without comment. 'She is always busy with her office, doesn't care for her old mother-in-law, doesn't care for her son', run the old lady's laments. As if the two of them – grandmother and grandchild – have done everything for themselves all these years: Rinti has grown to be twenty without any maternal care . . . the pacemaker in my mother-in-law's heart placed itself automatically and her cataract also removed itself! On its own. And all by itself, the Hindu annuity fund money reaches her as does her family pension. No one has to run around for them or stand in a queue. Nobody takes her to the doctor or the hospital, or fetches the medicines. Do her daughters come from Bombay and Durgapur to do all that? The older I grow, the wilder I get while witnessing human ingratitude! At least my parents aren't alive … just as well … had they been here, they too would have harboured a hundred reproaches against me. It simply isn't my luck to win hearts. Even after I have done so much for her through all these years, my mother-in-law tells her daughters to shift her to the 'Twilight Shelter' because her daughter-in-law doesn't take care. Who will bear the expenses? Her Hindu annuity fund and her pension will suffice. Perhaps they will. All right then, go, if that's what you want. Why should I interfere? Let her go. If Rinti too went away somewhere, it would be even better, I would move out into a working women's hostel and live in peace. I'm getting on too. I have only twelve years of service left. The 'Twilight Shelter' will also be my final destination. But no, not with my mother-in-law there! They have branches. I shall stay at another branch. I guess my mother-in-law will live at least for another ten years. She would then be eighty. Her daughters would have aged too. By then, who can tell, where they will be?

Rinti doesn't spend any time with his grandmother. I dislike that.

I really have no time myself. Cooking in the morning, then rushing off to the office, then doing my tuitions, then cooking again, and on top of that facing various other household hassles. I get no help from Rinti. He is busy with his practice in the field. Or else, he shuts himself up in his room, chatting with his friends or listening to cassettes of Western music. His contact with his grandmother is only when they watch TV together. Both of them are TV addicts. If he were to spend some time with her, talking to her, even if they were to compare notes sharing their grievances against me, may be then she wouldn't have wanted to go away to the 'Twilight Shelter'. What can I say – it is only natural for her to feel lonesome, being completely homebound. There is not much socializing in our family. The Salt Lake area seems like a faraway island. Only Rinti's friends visit us. Perhaps it wasn't a good move for my mother-in-law to leave the rented flat at Bhabanipur. But I managed to acquire this tiny flat with great difficulty, and finally we have a place we can call our own. Now we have our own flat but my mother-in-law wants to shift to the 'Twilight Shelter'. This may appear ironical and illogical, but it isn't actually so. What I don't understand is how, after we have been living together for twenty-five years, she still feels no affection or attachment towards me. When I lost my husband within five years of marriage, I joined the same office at the same post. It has been twenty years now. I have struggled hard to bring up our son. Though chronically ill, my mother-in-law helped me a lot through those early years, when Rinti was small. It was possible to take good care of him then because we lived in Bhabanipur. Our neighbours were closer than our own flesh and blood. The landlords never behaved like landlords. They were *Masima* and *Meshomoshai* to me and looked after little Rinti along with their own

grandchildren. The fact that Rinti's grandmother was at
home was an added reassurance. Sharing the same house,
same verandah, same courtyard – indeed Bhabanipur
was so convenient. Now, when I ask Rinti to visit
Bhabanipur and enquire after Masima – Meshomoshai
passed away two years ago – Rinti doesn't want to go.
He doesn't go. It surprises me. It's not easy to commute
all the way from Dalhousie to Bhabanipur, then again
from Bhabanipur to Salt Lake. But Rinti goes about the
city the whole day. Yet he won't visit them. Just because
he doesn't like to. Masima is getting on in age now, but
she lives happily surrounded by her sons, daughters-in-
law, and grandchildren. After we left, they re-arranged
those three rooms, in good taste. That's where her
grandson and his wife now stay. Masima knows the
art of keeping a family together. How many families
in Kolkata today can boast of living happily with three
sons, three daughters-in-law, grandsons, and their wives?
Certainly not my mother-in-law. She chews the happy
meal unhappily. Probably she finds this flat unlivable
because it belongs to me. I have bought it myself. The
flat where we lived earlier was rented in the name of
her late husband. She felt comfortable there. She finds
everything uncomfortable here. Even though this
accommodation is much better in comparison – much
more open and spacious. What a nice balcony! Nice

and airy. Jhilmil Amusement Park is next door. But Ma doesn't like anything here. There, the Ganga was close by. With the house being a single-storeyed bungalow, she could walk down every evening to the bank of the river and listen to the scriptures being read aloud. That's stopped now. She is not strong enough to go up and down the stairs too many times. Ma has no one to talk to, she has not made friends with our neighbours. She feels very lonely. That's a fact. In all fairness to her, I cannot really object if she wants to move to the 'Twilight Shelter'. She had asked Rinti to get her a form. He didn't. From what I understand, however reluctant I may be (I've lived my entire life against my wishes), since Rinti didn't oblige, it will be my unpleasant duty to get the form for her. Otherwise Grandma will start asking strangers from the neighbouring flats to do her this favour. Her daughters have gone back. No, they didn't get her the form either. But they said, 'If mother wishes to live without encumbrances at her old age, then why don't you arrange for that, Vandana? Since you have done everything for her, looked after her for so long – now if she …' But what will happen to Vandana when she retires and returns to her empty flat, no one thinks of that. I am forty-five or forty-six, my mother-in-law is seventy. I'll work for twelve-thirteen years more. The retirement benefits won't be too meagre.

This flat has been purchased on a housing loan. No one appreciates what I've done, instead, my mother-in-law is ready to leave the house any day. My son spends most of his time outside. Or, with his friends locked in his room in a cloud of smoke, Western music, and *adda*. There are girls in there as well as boys. This was not the practice in Bhabanipur. This is new to us, in Salt Lake. I have told him not to bring girls home. But Rinti doesn't listen. The grandmother's behaviour is incomprehensible – she doesn't seem to notice anything at all. She says nothing. As though she has no interest in the well-being of her grandson. But she should have opposed vehemently. And hats off to those girls! What about their parents? Have they nothing to say?

She is very shrewd. Expert at steering clear of trouble. When she goes away to the 'Twilight Shelter', as I know she will, then there'll be Rinti and I, just the two of us at home. Only Rinti, and his mother. It's not a good idea. My mother-in-law's presence surely had some significance. An elderly person being right there in the house for twenty-four hours – doesn't that have some value? At least, there is someone keeping an eye on the place. When I leave for office, there will be just Rinti at home. All by himself. The world of sports is not a very good one – the times are pretty bad too – I am very worried about Rinti.

'Twilight Shelter'
Five — Binapani

It is raining.

When it rains, this room is no longer a room here, but becomes a room in Hathibagan, the house where I grew up. The ceaseless torrents of rain and the soft white mist that gradually screens the greenery beyond, is exactly the way the cascade of my memories masks the present and keeps erasing the lived moment – I forget the place, the time; only the person remains. Just me and my past.

The rain had a different sound in my childhood. Or was the difference not really in the quality of the sound, but in the eagerness of my hearing? All my senses were keen then. All the colours were bright, every sound sharp, every touch meaningful. And now? Like the lotus in the evening, each faculty is closing down its petals one by one; the living world is turning opaque. Even the morning sun looks tired. No sight at all in the left eye. There is some vision in the right. I have to get the cataract operated – it must have matured by now. How much longer does it need? I'll soon be blind. My hearing is fading too. I can't hear very well unless spoken to loudly.

Those with whom I live, those who are my regular companions, find it hard to speak in a loud voice – except that Nistarini Devi. My goodness! She is a recent arrival, but what a voice! And what choice of subject matter for public discussion! A strange creature! Had I not lived to be seventy-five, I would have missed meeting this rare being. But if I live another ten years and stay in this same room, there is no way I can escape this Nistarini. Either she stays or I do. That woman manages to set fire even to my cooling, failing, gasping sensibilities. To describe her as uncultured is not enough. Uncivilized doesn't suffice either. I've never heard such language in my life. Never. Not even in Hathibagan. I have come here from Bhabanipur. And she has come, yes, from Rambagan. Romola, Zulekha, and others are planning an appeal to the management *to get rid of her.* People from Rambagan can't be allowed to stay here. She is poisoning the entire atmosphere. The lady doesn't lack money. She can stay all by herself in a separate flat. She has sufficient strength of body, mind, and wealth to supervise an army of domestic servants. Really, *she is a misfit here.* So restless about taking a dip in the Ganga, that every morning she must take a taxi to the river, accompanied by her ayah. How much money must one have to indulge in such luxuries? She has really *peculiar morals, not at all middle class. Quite a woman*! I think Salajnayani Bhattacharjee finds her intolerable yet she is so polite that she is unable to avoid her. Nistarini has caught hold of Pushpa Devi too. As her immediate neighbour staying in the adjoining room, she claims Pushpa Devi's friendship. Romola seems to be in the worst trouble. As it is, she hardly approves of anything, on top of that this lady has arrived, occupying an air-conditioned room, living in style. She has brought a lot of furniture, paintings, Chinese vases, her own TV, VCR, fridge, and furnished her room pretty well. Her son and daughter-in-law come to visit. They are completely Westernized in their ways. It is hard to believe that they belong to her family. They seem very cultured, their behaviour is extremely polite. That adjusting to her ways should be difficult for her son and daughter-in-law is not surprising at all. She had sent her son to Darjeeling and Delhi for his education. The daughter-in-law is also from Delhi. Both are much younger than my own sons. My eldest son is past fifty. These two are probably in their thirties. Nistarini doesn't seem to be sixty as yet – must have inflated her age to get a seat here. Very loud. And very crude. Perhaps she is the first illiterate inmate here.

It is raining.

In our Hathibagan house, the first rains used to fill the inner courtyard with a wonderful scent of damp earth. In our garden here, the season for *beli* and jasmine is almost over. It is now time for *kadam* and *keya* to bloom. But we don't have those plants in our garden here. There was a kadam tree in our Hathibagan house; a couple of keya shrubs too, by the pond. We were warned not to loiter near the keya shrubs, as snakes live there. The sound of the rain revives those scents – the strong fragrance of the keya flowers, the alluring aroma of the kadam florets. And the smell of someone's body. Whenever it rained, she used to run out into the terrace. And dance around to get drenched. She forgot that she was the daughter-in-law of a large joint family. Someone had once plucked a keya flower, for the first time in his life, just to gift it to her. Both his hands were torn by the thorns, he didn't have the know-how of plucking it. He also had a scolding from his father. You can't smuggle a keya flower into the house.

Father-in-law was seated in the baithak khana. He could see and he could smell it. But he merely scolded, didn't give him a thrashing. He didn't think that a mischief like picking a keya flower deserved a beating. The surprise, the amazement of the girl for whom the adventure was undertaken, and her pleasure in receiving the keya flower rises clearly in my heart. Her pleasure made the trouble he had taken worthwhile. Where is that youth who picked the keya flower? Where is that girl who loved to dance around in the rain?

A big terrace faced the room in the Hathibagan house, with the *thakurdalan* below. The two of us rushed around grappling on the terrace to collect the hailstones. He would have been seventy-five or seventy-six today had he lived. No point in thinking about that. Just as well that he is not alive. *Thakurpo* will remain young forever. There were no medicines for typhoid in those days. Thanks to chloromycetin, people do not die of typhoid any more.

Since I was not producing children, my father-in-law decided to engage a tutor and I began my studies at home. Thakurpo couldn't stop teasing me: 'Barren already at eighteen? Sejo Dada's going to marry again! Alas, Sejo Boudi, better pass IA and BA along with me, at least you can become a school-teacher and feed yourself!' Honestly, thank god that I did study! That's why I have retired as the principal of a government college. I had children too, when I was older. I had been much too thin earlier. My father-in-law saw his grandchildren as well as a daughter-in-law with a Master of Arts degree before he died. No, there aren't many families like the one I was married into. How many girls married at the age of eleven are encouraged to study, gain a masters degree, and work as the principal of a college? With the husband alive? Not a widow, nor a Brahmo – a married woman from an orthodox Hindu family whose generous father-in-law permitted her to study and reach the university level? My husband wasn't too keen. Fortunately, he lacked the will to openly oppose his father's decisions. He was always weak-willed. Thakurpo's enthusiasm pushed my education forward. But he died at the age of twenty-two. All through his life, my husband envied his brother. Jealous of his little dead brother! He used to say, 'You are the opposite of Rabi Thakur. Loving a dead brother-in-law all your life, you didn't care for the living husband.' He never realized that I loved him too. This fascination of mine with music – didn't that prove my love for him? Why he never understood that, remains a mystery to me. Didn't I start taking music lessons only because he was such a music lover? I learnt to play the esraj from him. I had hoped that music would build a bridge between the two of us; but that didn't happen. It didn't happen only because of his absurd jealousy. He is gone now and so is Thakurpo – his esraj keeps me company, I bear the legacy of his music, his sons have refused it. This intense and clear manifestation of my love did not touch him. My love for him and my love for Thakurpo are both true, but they are not the same thing. May be, because Thakurpo died, my love for him lives. Who knows whether it would have survived had he lived? In those days, we – let it be. No point in thinking about it.

The rain is reduced to a trickle. Parting the magic curtain of falling water, the plants and the trees are emerging like a green dream. The cloudy sky is melting into the distant lake – that the heart should continue to yearn for more than fifty years for one who went away at the age of twenty-two, is indeed very surprising. The fragrance of the keya flower, the scent of the damp earth, the sound of the rain, are all blended with my adolescence and that youth.

Arrey! What's that there? Isn't that a rainbow? After so many years! How beautiful!

'Twilight Shelter'
Six – Nistarini

Look here, *didi*, I brought this picture along; but do you know why I brought it? My grandfather-in-law got this done by a sahib painter. See this pink satin bed with this naked mem languishing in a voluptuous pose? Well, this seductive memsahib is my grandmother-in-law – hee-hee-hee, how's that? Why do you stare that way?

Grandmother-in-law means his *kept woman*, you know? Yes, yes, money's the master, in the name of money even golden-haired memsahibs rush and lie down in the lap of blackies. And why not? Will their colour fade if they do? My grandfather-in-law wasn't such a simple man. In those days, his father ran a business of salt and ice. But their main business was lending money to sahib companies. Like loan business? Just of a larger scope! Rich! He grew dirty rich. Then, whatever happens with so much money happened – my grandfather-in-law had each and every one of the vices. There was no vice on earth, no evil act that he didn't indulge in. Wine, women, hangers-on. In the middle of all that, my elder grandmother-in-law, his wife – he had married only once, very clever that way, – his wife brought up nine daughters and three sons, got the daughters married. My father-in-law was the eldest son. He took over his father's business, looked after everything. He wasn't skilled enough to keep twenty-thirty women like his father did. That needs real talent! What didn't his father, my grandfather-in-law, have in his pocket? Just that pink *mem*? He had *kafri* women too, with strong biceps, looking like Ma Kali, dark, tall, and big. Also Chinese and Japanese women like glass dolls. My mother-in-law saw them with her own eyes and I heard all this from her. The German woman looked like a fairy, it seems. Kashmiri women, Madrasi women, *baiji*s from Lucknow – was there any place from where he didn't get his women? From all over. He had his agents everywhere. He would get hold of any beautiful girl he fancied. It was his habit to keep women.

My father-in-law wasn't that sort. He perhaps grew disgusted watching his father. A calm and quiet man, not a lion among men, and had no time to waste on wine and women. He was busy looking after the property. My grandfather-in-law gifted each one of his women a whole house! Can you imagine that, didi? The three sons were finally left with only four houses. The brothers ate from a single kitchen and lived under their mother's *anchal*. Soon Ma Lakshmi smiled on their business and four houses became twelve. Then grandmother-in-law herself divided the property, gave four houses, and a separate kitchen to each brother. When I was married, I saw four houses. I saw my grandmother-in-law too. She closed her eyes soon after my wedding. My father-in-law treated me like his daughter, the son was useless – I mean my husband – too much spoiling had made him less than human. He drowned himself in alcohol and amused himself with prostitutes in the outhouse. What did he know about business – he also happened to be slow-witted. But being slow doesn't mean that he can't be a debauch, does it? Father-in-law increased the property and built seven houses, but he registered them all in my name. My mother-in-law was a simple woman. I was married at the age of eight, and she treated me

like a child of her womb, never subjecting me to the
tiniest ill-treatment. I was the apple of their eyes. My
father-in-law personally trained me, taught me how to
look after the property, and care for the business, how to
make it grow; the son knew only how to blow and burn.
My mother-in-law had given birth to more children but
none of them survived. Because he was the only living
offspring, no one said anything to him. Well, to 'continue
the family line' the son was married off – but who'll
do the continuing? The son didn't have that capacity at
all. But leave all that! After all I have shown the faces
of grandchildren to my father-in-law! Who cares whose
capacity it was – if an illiterate woman like me can make
the houses grow from seven to thirteen, will I have any
trouble with an impotent husband? Is there a shortage
of men in the world? How could seven houses become
thirteen? By working to death. But the actions of a
woman are slightly different from those of a man. As
you see me today, didi, I look like a witch. But this is
not how I used to be! True I was no heavenly beauty, no
pomegranate-seed princess; my complexion wasn't that of
the *champa* blossom but of the *safeda* fruit. But people
don't eat the flower, do they? They prefer the ripe and
juicy fruit. I was a juicy little fruit. I had what you call
'the real stuff ', you know? For which men fall at your
feet like obedient puppies – that's the kind of 'stuff ' I

had. The wealthiest and the most powerful men of the town came fawning at my feet. Why six, had I wished, I could've built fifty palaces not only in Kolkata, or Delhi, or Bombay, but in Dhaka and Rangoon as well. Who didn't visit my house? When a flower blooms and its scent spreads, bees come thronging. Well, my scent also spread. But I wasn't greedy. I stopped with six houses, a woman shouldn't grow too much, there's no need to surpass your father-in-law. Who knows Ma Lakshmi might be unhappy at that? That's why six, just one less than what my father-in-law left, deliberately one. So it doesn't look like I'm trying to surpass my father-in-law. You're from our generation, didi, you'll surely understand. My son and daughter-in-law – they can't. They're lost in competition, trying to win races. *Arrey baba*, that to lose willingly, with a purpose, is also a kind of victory, won't enter their heads.

Look at the girls today. Do they know how to trap men? No, they don't. If your entire stomach and back are exposed, even the bellybutton is bared, shamelessly showing off half of your naked breasts, and letting the anchal slither off your chest to trail at your knees – is that the way to hunt down men? It only gives them extra pleasure. If they get everything for free, why exert? But what does the woman gain? Didi, those who play the game, know the rules of man-hunting, those who don't, can neither learn nor be taught. It's possible to kill men fully covered from head to foot with a burqa; but one must know the tricks of hunting. That Zulekha-di? She knows. She has the skill. She'll know what I'm talking about. That's the stuff I had. You know how the saying goes: flirting behind the veil? That's it. Our time was like that. We'd pull the veil on the face down to the chest, but underneath the sari there wouldn't even be a petticoat to cover the naked bottom. I heard stories of the chicks of the baniya families painting their buttocks with *alta*, then wrapping the thinnest of Begumbahar saris around, just one layer, and taking a walk on the terrace, showing off their plump red behinds like monkeys. Not seen that myself, though. But I still don't wear a petticoat. Who'll wear petticoats? Those who've faults in their figure or have something to hide. You all are educated women, sister, you'll call me a vulgar, shameless, immodest broad. Doesn't wear a petticoat. But, sister, the body's a gift of God. If it's good, worth showing others, then shouldn't it be shown? Should it be kept for one person's use alone and be wasted? Is that fair? Will that please God? You tell me, sister, you've read books, shouldn't good things be shared with many?

My body was a gun and my eyes were its triggers. My glances took aim and pulled the triggers, the body shot its bullets. After that, no matter how big a man, the bloke was sure to die. Haven't I seen enough in this life? Mostly just a peep show would do. But with a more experienced prey, that wouldn't be enough, you needed a different trick. Oh yes, I sure knew how to sleep with a man! Was it like the bimbos of today? Eat to the full, change into some skimpy nylon skirt, some unwashed rag, yank the bedcover, fix the mosquito-net, switch off the light, smear dabs of white cream on the face looking like a ghoul, and lie down beside your husband! And the husband? Blindly guessing and groping about in the dark, and finishing off the job at hand. Then they snore away peacefully. No, dear. That won't do. Are we cats and dogs or what? During winter, I used to break a bottle of imported perfume every night and empty it on the bed. Every night. In summer, the top of the mosquito-net was strewn with plenty of fragrant jasmine flowers. The posts of the four-poster were twined with jasmine garlands, and in each corner of the room, I burnt a bunch of sandal incense. Oh, what heavenly fragrance! One lamp should be allowed to remain lit at that hour, only to be blown out just before falling asleep – but not a moment before that. What's the use of beauty if it isn't seen? He'll then imagine you to be whoever he wants in bed. No way! That can't happen. He must see with whom he is sleeping. One soft light must burn in the corner. I used to come to bed wearing a breezy fine snowy white muslin sari with a dashing red border loosely wrapped around, and my whole body jingling with jewellery. Every part of my body, every limb decorated with ornaments. From the parting in my hair, to my little toe – a jewel for every part. The lover carefully removes each ornament and grows impatient – that's the trick, you understand? Keep him waiting, as long as you can, that's the game.

Can you enjoy the game fully in the very same place every time? You can't. It's necessary to change the venue from time to time. So, sometimes we would go to the terrace. There were pots of beli flowers and jasmine creepers along the trellis – their scent on moonlit summer nights was strong and heady – unbelievable. So beautiful! At midnight, we spread the mat on the floor and covered it with wet khus-khus and soft cushions – if the lover was Kamal Shil, he sat near my feet and played the surbahar (I had a small *zari morha* on which I sat). If he was Bamacharan Sadhukhan, he played the esraj, but if he was the tabla player Ramlal Mishra, hee-hee-hee, then, of course, there was no musical session! Every single night with your lover must feel like the wedding night. Rushing in and lying down, is there any fun in that? Can love-making be like gorging? It can't. That's the way coolies mix and gobble their *chhattu* on the street. Finishing the basic job of filling the stomach, satisfying hunger. Does the Bengali gentleman eat that way?

Doesn't he need the entire spread of *panchabyanjan*, all five tastes in his sumptuous meals? From the bitter to the sweet? Doesn't he enjoy being fanned while he eats? And the box of paan in the end? Love-making's like that. One must pay attention to it, devote time, make careful calculations, dress up for it, and create the proper mood. Make no effort yet acquire the best result? No, sir! Things don't happen that way. Just as rituals must be observed for worshipping a deity, so details must be attended to for making love. Lovemaking has its own rituals. One must learn all the rituals, all the tricks. Only then will men remain collared and chained like a pet dog. After all, youth is short-lived – how many days does it last? Is it right to spend it all on one person? The more people you can share it with, the greater will be your own enjoyment – better to make the best use of it. There're so many types of men in the world – unless you get them into bed you can't make out who they really are. Man's the king in the outside world; woman's the king in bed, that is, if she knows how to rule. One must know. Nistarini Choudhury knows. Nistarini was never a straight and simple woman, and she isn't one now. In my time, one couldn't afford to be scatterbrained like my daughter-in-law. My husband was no man. Not only was he a drunkard, but he had also developed the habit of spending all his time lying around with sluts, right from his boyhood days. Plus being a fool. No sense at all. How'd I manage with such a man? Well, my father-in-law was a noble soul, a very good man. So that his stupid son doesn't blow away the ancestral property, he had legally transferred everything, all his property, in my name. All these children that I have – do you think all of them have the same father? Unhuh, only I know which one is whose. Huh, my father-in-law's bloodline continues! For sure! But it pleased my father-in-law. My husband – poor man – didn't possess that capacity. Had Nistarini been a different sort of a woman, how would his family line continue? It was possible only because of me. It's all my doing. My father-in-law knew everything, but said nothing. What could he say? Wasn't he aware of his own son's flaw? But to tell you the truth, I wasn't sorry that my stupid husband didn't come home. There was never a shortage of men in my life. Even after losing five children, as God willed, I'm still the mother of a son and two daughters. My daughters are like Lakshmi incarnate; my son too is highly qualified, he's a big officer. But, didi, my son has become a sahib. I sent him to a missionary school in Darjeeling – the home situation was such a mess, I didn't want him to see all that. Besides, the place, after all, was Rambagan. How long does it take a young man to go astray? Suppose he had followed his father's path?

My husband died a long time ago, and it's been five years since Bhattacharjee Moshai passed away. His son Kanto manages the business and performs the daily puja, the regular rituals for the family deity. Excellent boy, Kanto. Bhattacharjee Moshai was our money manager and family priest. Part of the money's put in *debottar* trust for the family deity. What an incredible man he was, sister, it's difficult to explain – Bhattacharjee Moshai – but let that be, no point in talking of him. A noble soul, he's in heaven, in the lap of God. See this silver paan box here, want to know who gave me this? The Raja of Pikepara! And that pair of Chinese vases? Didn't you notice them in the corner of my room? Those are mine. Benu Mallik of Pathuriyghata gave them to me once during puja, full of flowers. I've brought them along. I recall everything looking at them. Yes, the women were surely valued in Calcutta in our days! Women today can't even imagine such attention. These days men have a feast for their eyes for free; they see the women cavorting around baring their bodies up to their navels. Keeping everything covered, we used to hand out only a little at a time. The hunger must be kept alive, desire must be urged on, the wick sharpened. If the hunger's easily satisfied, why would they come fawning at your feet? Move a finger and beckon, and watch the men come running to you, wagging their tails. You must take care of your body, and keep it ready. Should you sell your stuff like vegetable vendors, pouring yourself out onto the market floor, and soliciting customers? Must women be greedy like that? That cheapens you, and gives men the upper hand. No wonder they have learnt to haggle. Nonsense, I say! All this education has spoilt the women's minds, ruined their luck, and cheapened their market value. Men and women have the same value today – like rice crispies and sugar crystals being priced the same. How long can dharma tolerate this? Earlier, a woman's mind was a precious thing, like a fragile wine glass – the slightest carelessness and it would shatter – must be handled cautiously, a rough touch could crack it – but now? The woman's mind is like a rubber band – pull it, drag it, and nothing happens. Rough and tough. Men have all the fun.

Could the men dare to behave this way during our time? Men are rascals by nature. Ungrateful lot. They should be made to run around the mill, and strung through their noses, only then they remain loyal. Show a little softness, and they sit upon your head. It's the kingdom of heaven for men these days, women have built their own pyres. The ghomta was a very good thing, my dear, it took much cajoling and pleading to lift the veil for a rare glimpse of the face – now the entire body is clearly in view. Easily, without charge! Why, look at the neckline of your own blouse, Romola-di, at your age? And beneath the blouse, the naked midriff? Is that quite proper, my dear? What did I say, the hunger must be kept burning, never quench it in full!

Aparajita's Narrative

Just waiting now.

Waiting patiently for that inevitable moment. I thought senility was a terrible disease, thought aging to be an unbearable condition. After a lifetime of ability and activity, to be imprisoned all of a sudden into a state of inability and inactivity is simply unbearable! Youth snaps its fingers at the incapacities of childhood. Then comes middle age. No, it has neither deer-like agility nor elephantine majesty. It comes like a python. And beyond the autumn world of the middle age lies the realm of winter. Here, in the still world of snow, one needs to generate one's own warmth. That warmth can be drawn from the accumulations of one's entire lifetime. In the kingdom of snow, only the breath of life brings warmth. The coldness of old age can be transcended with the warmth of one's own heart and soul. The treasury of the heart, the treasury of the intellect, the treasury of faith. Sometimes even the accumulations of habit can contribute something.

With age, the control over your mind enhances, but the control over the nuts and bolts of your body loosens, and growing lax, they can become a source of embarrassment. The other day, I read in Madame de Beauvoir's memoirs that in his old age, Sartre, her lifelong companion, had lost some muscular control, causing incontinence. But he hadn't lost an iota of control over his mind and intellect. That could be more painful. The mind scolds, 'Shame on you, what's this!' The body answers, 'What can I do? I can't help it!'

Day by day, our relationship with the earth becomes more complicated. During childhood, when each fresh sensibility is opening its doors and windows one by one, a simple and natural relationship develops with the earth – which changes subtly in old age, when nature starts locking up the doors and windows of each of those sense organs one by one. The home and the threshold are blurred, darkness descends, and shadows lengthen in the woods. This is an awful shadow. The night that falls after this dusk, has no dawn. The first dawn of creation and its last night – the creator keeps distinct for each one of us. For some it is stormy; for some, there might be a terrible drought. For some, the southern breeze, and for some, the icy winds blow.

For each of us, the earth has a separate arrangement, prepares a different basket of offering. The stars and the planets get to know each one of us, holding a separate light over our faces. Again illuminating each path with a separate light, they show us our way home.

The junction-station is past. The destination is not too far. The eyes are eager to go. The ears are ready to leave. The heart says, I've had enough, I want no more. The body too has sent signals for departure, there mightn't be further need to continue the homeopath's treatment for three years.

I'm happy to be in this group of vanaprasthees. After accomplishing their life's work, the retired people have finally found freedom from work. Free! Free! Free! The housewives have no housework. The salaried have no office. Can there be a more satisfying time? Now is the time to reflect. Think. Just think. Dive down into the depths of your mind. Swim around in the bottomless ocean of memory. Bring up pearls. Gather gems.

Many of my companions have begun to lose their memories. I'm sad for them. My eyes are going. Ears are going. Legs are gone. Let them go. I still have my mind. And my constant companion, my childhood friend, my memory has not deserted me. Reasoning and logic haven't abandoned me either. As long as I have them, I am alive. I am human. Sartre was alive till the very end, and he lived as a complete human being though he might have lost muscular control for some of those years. The ego gets hurt. One has to become somewhat dependent on others. But that's nothing. That's not the gravest loss that aging and senility can bring. Such things can happen to younger people as well, in times of illness. One would naturally feel embarrassed to wet the bed, but that's nothing to feel frustrated about because that's not the defeat of the human being, it is the failure of the animal. It had nothing to do with the thinker, the philosopher that Sartre was. At least, that's what I feel. At the age at which I am now, Sartre was already dead, his dearest companion had also passed away before reaching this age. I liked him very much. No, I never met him. I have never visited France and he had never come to Kolkata. Yet I know him well. I've read his books. Almost all of them. The trouble I took to learn English has been fruitful. He was younger to me. But was far more experienced. He had the opportunity to read much more, to travel around. To see this world.

Experience is real wisdom. Experience is age. Many things we learn in life are wrongly learnt. Many things learnt through life turn topsy turvy in old age. What we have coveted all our life as a valuable metal bowl, old age reveals it to be a worthless clay pot. And that too, not hardened through fire but unbaked and insubstantial. Left to get wet in the rain, it could melt and disappear – not just its bright golden paint but the whole entity.

It doesn't last. Nothing lasts – not these unbaked clay forms – yet they stood proudly through the years with the false permanence of metal! Alas, human relationships!

I have reached old age, then! I can't get over this surprise. I always thought that I would never age, that my life would end long before that. A soothsayer had said that I wouldn't live long. That's why though I was a girl child, I hadn't been neglected by my parents. A child with a short life, not expected to live long. Had she known that her short-lived daughter would be racing to touch the nineties, my mother's attitude would have been different, I know. Well, mother herself had a short life – she left us at fifty-six, with her head in her husband's lap. She didn't reach old age. A grandmother only in name, she was totally capable and as active as a young woman. The grandchildren were all growing up under her care. Mother didn't know that her life would be short. She had many dreams and desires, which remained unfulfilled.

Mother didn't reach it, but her carefully tended daughter has reached old age. Age is like running a marathon race. Those of us, who have crossed eighty and are moving towards ninety, are the winners. Who could have guessed that even old age would hold such surprises? No, Rabindranath knew it. He had in his collection a whole array of varied emotional experiences of the old age, bitter, sweet, pungent, sour. And he has shared as much as he could with us. Poems that had made no sense to me when I was young, are clear to me now:

> In the densely crafted heap of hard stones
> I can see his unattainable form from a distance
> I have crossed the perilous paths
> As I come close my mind becomes clear of the illusions
>
> Here, the sky extends a cordial welcome
> Here, the breeze hugs me like an old friend
> In this unknown land a known voice rings
> Opening up the door to my family home.

'Twilight Shelter'
Seven — Sarasi

Today Khoka came. *Baro Khoka*.

There's nothing to say. *Bauma's* sense of duty is impeccable, every week someone or the other comes to find out if I need something. My clothes are regularly brought back from home, properly washed and ironed. No one visits me without a box of sweets. But Khoka's coming was different.

Khoka doesn't come here. He doesn't get the time to come. He has so much to do. Delhi today, Bombay tomorrow, Hong Kong the day after, and New York the next. When does he have the time? How much time does Bauma get to spend with him, for that matter? Only when the two of them attend parties together, perhaps they talk in the car while they drive along. Otherwise, it's usually very late by the time Khoka returns home. Bauma can't stay awake that late every day. The children have school – she has to leave home very early every morning. I used to take them when I was at home. Does anybody keep him company now when Khoka sits down for a meal? May be Kalipada supervises it. Every week, Bauma sends Kalipada here with all the news if she is unable to visit herself.

It is not that I feel less happy to see Kalipada instead of Bauma. Kalipada has been with us from my husband's time. For how many years have the daughters-in-law been in the family? *Chhoto Bauma* doesn't come too often. She stays in Salt Lake. Very far away. It's like going from one end to the other. And *Chhoto Khoka*? The less said about him, the better. At least, Chhoto Bauma has visited a few times. She may be from Punjab, but she's quite a nice girl. Chhoto Khoka hasn't come even once. At least come once out of curiosity, to know for yourself what sort of a place this 'Twilight Shelter' is – but no, not even that. From the beginning, he was adamant: 'No, Ma mustn't go!' But Ma did. That was it. He was mad. Just like his father, is Chhoto Khoka. Stubborn, short tempered but not bad at heart. Father's son.

Khoka is different.

He is like *my* father. Much too good-natured. Too good. But follows his wife's directions to the syllable. The way my father used to be. Whatever mother said was final. That ensured peace in the household. Khoka knows nothing beyond his wife. It isn't easy to find a dutiful wife like Bauma these days. She has a careful eye on everything. Nothing must be amiss. I had no problem at all. Chhoto Khoka and Chhoto Bauma have a small two-bedroom flat. How eager, how determined they were to fit me into that small space. I didn't agree. Living like that doesn't quite suit me. Here, I have a single room and I am fine. To live under *Baro Bauma*'s controlled generosity, no matter how much care she takes of me, doesn't suit me. And Baro Bauma's nature! As long as she is around, no one else can be the mistress in the house. After giving it a serious thought, I decided to rent out the house and move in here. Baro Khoka has a huge flat from his office; Chhoto Khoka has that tiny flat, his father-in-law purchased it in his wife's name. I could't possibly live all by myself in that big place – nor did I wish to become a burden on my children. Baro Khoka can't be expected to live in that narrow Shyam Bazar lane, considering the high official position he holds. No matter how large his ancestral home at Madan Mitter Lane is, the kind of people he has to socialize with cannot be entertained there. It is difficult even for a large car to enter our lane.

When Khoka and Bauma moved away to their Ballygunj flat, I didn't want to stay on all by myself in Madan Mitter Lane. Chhoto Khoka was still in Delhi. He is in Kolkata now, but no one knows when and where he'll fly away again. They are childless, so they are not bound by the fixed routines of schools and colleges. He is an artist. Chhoto Bauma also paints. They have just one large room. That's their studio. The other serves as both the bedroom and dining area. They were dying to accommodate me within that small space. Amazing! They were saying they would sleep in the studio itself. There's a pair of low platform beds in that room. They put up their friends there. Crazy! Crazy! Though a Punjabi, Krishna is a wonderful girl. I had wondered, after all, a non-Bengali daughter-in-law, who knows how she would be? But Krishna is as simple-hearted as a child. Has a wonderful open laughter, and is very straightforward. Her eyes fill with tears at the slightest hurt. Perhaps no one else would have suited Chhoto Khoka better. She weeps at his headstrongness, but doesn't quarrel. That makes him feel ashamed and he softens. Its quite nice to spend a day at their Salt Lake flat.

The view of the sunset from their kitchen is astounding. Krishna showed it to me once. I haven't visited Salt Lake for nearly eight or nine months, ever since I've come here. Its been eight or nine months now that I have seen Chhoto Khoka's face. Nor has he seen his mother's. It seems he's still mad with rage. What a boy!

Baro Khoka came today.

He has got another promotion. He came to seek my blessings, to do a *pronam*. That Bauma didn't come along was a great surprise. Bauma constantly guards Khoka like the police. Even after ten years of marriage, she doesn't understand me. Even if I were alone with Khoka, I would never say anything to my son that I wouldn't say in front of her. After marriage, the son is no longer someone with whom the mother can share everything freely. To speak to the son means also speaking to his wife. Whether she is physically accompanying him or not, the wife is always subtly present. Even if my daughters-in-law do not realize this, I do. Even otherwise, what could I say about Bauma, who is so dutiful? In fact, I would prefer her to be less dutiful – that's all I can say! Because of her nature, not only is there cordiality between the two daughters-in-law, but her relations with her sisters-in-law are also remarkable. On pujo, *bhai phota*, and birthdays, she buys them three expensive saris. On wedding anniversaries, she buys expensive presents for both husband and wife. My Bauma never forgets the date and the year for any important event. Everything is noted down in her diary. And Chhoto Bauma is just the opposite – doesn't remember a thing. She even forgets Chhoto Khoka's birthday sometimes!

Two sons. Two daughters. All have suitable homes and suitable partners. Is there anything for me to do at home? This is better. Actually, this is the best arrangement, this new home. Here, we make all sorts of handicrafts, whatever we know. Everything is collected and the money made from their sale goes to the Naree Seva Ashram where many poor women live. It is a charitable Home, unlike ours. This long human life was spent serving the interests of family and relatives. Let's see if the remainder can be spent in the service of others.

Khoka came today.

What he means to me, the place he holds in my heart, only Bauma can understand. And because she knows it, she doesn't let him come too often or too near. Stops him under various excuses and keeps him away from me. If she hadn't been down with fever today, she would certainly have come with him. She understands, but Khoka doesn't. What does he know of the ways of life? How does such a simple person manage such complicated situations in his office, I wonder!

Khoka is like my father. Quiet, good-natured, a devoted worker. Happy to leave the entire responsibility of his children and mother to his wife. But yes, his wife is capable; she neglects nothing. Office, office, office! Perhaps because she can manage so beautifully, Khoka can't. Can't? Or, doesn't? When his father died suddenly after three days of illness, didn't Khoka manage everything? He took on all the responsibility. Guided the household with strong hands. Completed his studies in the evening shift while working during daytime. My brother placed him into a chartered accountancy firm – after that Khoka has only tasted success.

Khoka is forty-four now.

Oh, that Khoka. Rain water used to collect in the slit trenches dug during the war. Tumbling into the water, how he would romp about in it, 'bathing' in joy, and shouting 'River! River!' I bet no one could get more pleasure on the beaches of Puri-Digha-Gopalpur than what Khoka and his little friends used to get messing around in those muddy holes! Today's Khoka is a refined gentleman. He was always a calm and quiet boy anyway. Chhoto Khoka was the incorrigibly disobedient one. Always discontented. He was always naughty and remains so even today.

Today Khoka wandered around and inspected the garden. 'Look, Ma, your favourite *shiuli* tree.' Thank goodness, at least he still remembers his mother's favourite flower. Khoka looked at my room, the verandah, the pitcher with the glass, the clothes-hanger.

He looked at the empty white walls. He said, 'Must send you some pictures, Ma, the walls are too bare.'

Khoka, you can't see within my heart, son – it is not a bare wall at all – it is packed full of pictures, like an album. Turn the pages, as long as you want, its pages will never come to an end!

'Twilight Shelter'
Eight – Romola

My husband was a barrister. Barrister J.C. Mitter. We had a huge house at Chaurangi Terrace. His chamber was in the house. Neither of our sons studied law. Both of them are engineers and settled in America. No, the daughter didn't study law either. She studied social psychology and now teaches in Bombay. The son-in-law is a lawyer. So, the father-in-law's library has been of some use to him. But I couldn't keep the house. He didn't leave a will, you see. There were three houses. I sold them all – after the sales, the children divided the proceeds with me. Each of them has bought a flat. The sons have leased out theirs. The daughter lives in hers. I? No, what will I do with a flat? How can I live alone? There are many problems at my age. I deliberately avoided keeping a flat.

This is much better. An old age home is the right place for me. I like people. I'm a gregarious person. Sitting alone reading a book, or watching TV in an empty flat – the way old people live in Britain, that's not for me! Neither can I keep pets. I have no love for dogs and cats. Old memsahibs spend their last days serving their pets.

And our old Hindu women adopt gods. How many gods they have! Shelves full of them. Rooms full of them. They bathe them, feed them, dress them, sing to them, and much more. The rituals of worship, scent and incense, bells and conch shells – such paraphernalia fill twenty hours of their day. Or else, there are gurus and godmen. This *gurudeb* or that *guruma*. They too have their own special cultural programmes and social functions. The old people are kept pretty busy. There could be Bhagavat reading or Gita interpretation, *Harir loot*, and Sai bhajan or a four month long spiritual occupation, *chaturmasya naam gaan*. In this country, there are various kinds of traditional entertainment available to the old people, other than the TV or the radio. They provide spiritual and intellectual stimulation. Such things are lacking somewhat in Western cultures. Of course, I was no believer in idolatry. Being a barrister, my husband had no patience for these Hindu rituals. We never became Brahmos formally though, and Hindu practices are still observed in our family for weddings and funerals. It was just that my husband couldn't tolerate such religious orthodoxy, he considered it as fanaticism. I argued that religion improves morals, promotes ethical development. He would say that the maximum number of wars in world history were fought over religion; it actually destroys your morals, and blinds your conscience. That's what he said. I don't know, I always followed what he said. I find these days rather difficult, I feel very lonely. He was ten years older than me. He would be seventy-six now, had he lived. But he was young and energetic, and left us suddenly. He had gone to Delhi to argue a case in the Supreme Court, he didn't walk back home. Stroke. Both our sons were abroad and one daughter was not yet married then. She was studying in Bombay at the Tata Institute of Social Sciences (TISS) and I was alone in Kolkata. I flew to Delhi as soon as I heard but it was all over by then. Our daughter also joined me…. Anyway, let those things be.

I've lived here for six years now.

See this talcum powder that I use? My son's gift; he has given me a dozen cakes of Camay soap. For the entire year. What a lovely fragrance. His mem wife has a good heart. Much better than the elder daughter-in-law. She is the one to send me gifts now and then. I looked around for a good match and arranged the marriage of my elder son. A convent educated girl. But the daughter-in-law hasn't been a good choice. Very selfish. Keeps her mother-in-law and sister-in-law at arm's length.

And the son-in-law? He is a fine boy. A lawyer. But a Maharashtrian. My daughter lives in a beautiful flat in Bombay. She has taken her father's library to Bombay.

No one has a flat in Kolkata. The sons bought theirs in Delhi. The daughter bought her's in Bombay.

I live here. I was born and brought up here, in Kolkata. I can't be relaxed living in Delhi or Bombay, away from Kolkata. I have visited my sons of course, in Canada, and in America. One lives in Calgary and the other in New Jersey. Not close at all. Three thousand miles or something is the distance, but the telephone is a great boon. Science can reduce all distance in a matter of seconds.

My husband was a barrister, my father was a judge in Calcutta High Court, and my maternal uncle was MP Bhuvan Gupta. One of my cousins runs a big business in Singapore. His father-in-law belongs to that place. Tamil-speaking. Both of us visited them once. That was long before the VCR and all were invented. Or we could have bought those. They are extremely rich and own almost half of Singapore. What a fabulous house! And what fantastic furniture! Why should they want to return to Kolkata? What do they have here? I returned – but that's a different matter. My entire life is here. Why live out my life beyond the oceans? The sons and their wives have their work. The grandchildren are in their schools. I sit alone in front of the TV all day long. Or else, the son and daughter-in-law will return after work, so I cook and keep things ready for them. How can I stay home the whole day, doing nothing and not even do that tiny bit for them? Doesn't look nice. Yet, I don't enjoy it. I've never done any housework in my life. I can't become a cook in my old age! I'm far better off here in Kolkata. But yes, this cowshed has many problems. The food is bad and so is the service. And the company? Well, you have to be very selective. There are both the good and the bad. A mixed bag. An awful woman has arrived recently, and lives in an air-conditioned room, with a private ayah, private TV, fridge, VCR, and the whole lot. I've never ever seen anyone like her! She's a horror! What vocabulary! What topics of conversation! Quite incredible! Then there is another lady on the other side who has no control over her body – she wets herself, wanders into the music room in soiled clothes, with hair all tangled like a mad woman's. She's totally senile. Such creatures give a bad name to the place. Binapani-di used to be the principal of Bethune College. I told her about the dirty language of that other woman, but she laughed it off, saying, 'At this age need we fear bad company? So what if she speaks that way?'

'Twilight Shelter'
Nine — Nistarini

I'm here of my own will – what else! Never in my life have I allowed others' will to be forced upon me. Everything I do, is just as I wish, always. Yes. Tutu's my only son – after all the others died, he was the only one, the last light of my father-in-law's family. But did I have a chance to keep that son close to me? If the boy spends his entire life in the sahibs' schools, does he remain your own child any more? No. He's not a bad sort though, an honest soul, a decent boy, doesn't ill-treat his mother or disrespect her. I never learnt to read and write. My father got rid of me early, marrying me off as a half-naked kid. Living at my in-laws' place was like playing in a doll's house. My son could have scorned me – I had no education, after all – and my son is so learned! No, he'd never do that. But, yes, he did marry according to his own wish. The choice was his own, but a beautiful bride, from just the right family, a suitable match in every way. And a graduate too. A graduate daughter-in-law, she speaks in English half the time. That way she suits my son's needs. But what of that? I'm like poison in her eyes. She can't bear her ma-in-law. And how can she? She's half a memsahib herself. Her mother found her freedom early, she died, leaving behind the three-year old. Since then she's been in mem schools. Has become a mem herself. What can you expect? Pollutes everything in the house with her lawless, mlechcha practices. How long can I bear all that disorderly conduct, tell me, didi? There would be arguments and disputes between the two of us. And guess who suffered? Tutu, poor thing, would be caught like a thief in between, With his mother on one side and wife on the other. He must listen to both, keep both sides happy. Tutu, poor thing, is never relaxed, always tense. Stays away from home most of the time, rushing off to Delhi or Bombay. Finally, I thought, no, this can't go on. I must decide this way or that. Constantly pulled between the mother and the wife, my boy's life is withering away in the tension. What if he developed some chest trouble? Like his father who was felled by a single attack – gone. Anxiety had damaged his heart. He himself was entirely to blame, of course. He was like a thief with his father and a thief with his wife. I was totally shaped by his father. How much contact did I have with my husband? He lived by his own rules, and I by mine. That doesn't mean that there was a shortage of men in Nistarini's life! Never. They hung around me like leeches as long as I had my looks and my body, as long as I was a young woman. Did I visit the *birthing chamber* nine times just like that? But what was I saying? Yes, Bauma rushes off to her father's house in her anger. To sulk in her *sulking chamber*! My son feels miserable without her. He'd bring her back on his own in a few days. Lately, I didn't quite like her ways. A modern girl. She has a tongue; she has beauty; she can read and write. How long would it take her to catch another husband? But Tutu is quiet and shy, totally devoted to his wife – it would break his heart. What to do? So I made a plan to gauge Tutu's mind. No one can beat Nistarini in diplomatic planning. Married into a baniya-family, I've witnessed so much! Bauma's cousin sister came to visit one day; she has placed her mother in some old women's home. The old woman refuses to stay at her son-in-law's, nor can she live alone. The cousin told me that her memsahib sister couldn't stand my Rambagan vocabulary and had decided to go away forever to her father's place, leaving even her husband if need be. She said, 'Listen, Masima, I can't stop her. See if you can.' Well, there aren't too many things in this world that Nistarini Choudhury can't do. I told her, 'Don't worry at all. I'll do whatever needs to be done. Let Tutu come back.' When Tutu came home, in order to know his mind, I went to him and made up a story, 'Tutu, my son, I've been stuck in this house for years and years, I want to go on a pilgrimage. I told Bauma. I leave on akshay tritiya day.' So Tutu said, 'Where are you going, Ma? Who's going with you? How long will you be away?' I said, 'Son, I won't lie to you. I told Bau that I'm going on a pilgrimage. Actually, I'm going to an ashram-like place meant for old people. By depositing money, one gets an air-conditioned room there with separate bath and toilet, five meals a day. The vegetarian kitchen is very clean; with a special arrangement for widows; they take care of the medical treatment in case of illness. You don't have to worry at all. Your mem-wife can't stand my Rambagan language. You better live here with your wife in this house of your ancestors. That will be the right thing to do. Let me go for some time and check what sort of a place that one is. Kanto has found out for me, there are not one or two but eight or nine such places. Here. Among them, the most comfortable place is also the most expensive. But that's only normal – you have to pay for what you get, whether it's in the guru's ashram or in the prostitute's cabin. This one's like a boarding house for old people. Business-like arrangement, not like an orphanage for the elderly orphans, but rooms with telephones at two thousand rupees a month. I've paid twenty-five thousand rupees as deposit. Many such ashrams have been built for the aged. Your wife's cousin has put her mother in one. She is Bouma's Mamima. That made me think: let me find out. Let me see what sort of arrangement this is. No one goes off to Kashi these days. Most live under their children's control. That Nistarini won't need to do; nor will Nistarini go to Kashi.

My Uma-Roma-Tutu are here, my grandchildren are all in Kolkata, Kanto and Baro Bouma are here – leaving them all, why Kashi, I don't even wish to go to heaven. So I've fixed everything, I've fixed an auspicious day also; I shift to the shelter on Akshay Tritiya day. You won't stop me, will you, son? I've lived in this house for fifty-sixty years; I need a change of place now.' What can I say, didi, my heart breaks to think of it, my son kept his mouth shut. He stood still, like a deaf and dumb creature. Not once did he utter, 'No Ma, don't go. Ma, please stay.' Then, I knew his mind. When my son doesn't want me there, then what is home to me? I was dejected.

Immediately, I gave Kanto the money. In two instalments. Kanto fixed up the room. Really, didi, isn't this a beautiful room? This open verandah, the grass, the trees, the park, such a breezy seventh-floor room, – going up and down in a lift, could Rambagan give me such things in seven generations? Kanto came and reported to me that there's no other problem at home, except that only one kitchen works now, with separate vegetarian and non-vegetarian ovens. What else? Here, in my room I have a fridge, a phone, my own TV. A personal maid for one hundred and fifty rupees extra every month. That's why I brought Mokkhada along. It's only one and half weeks since I came. Haven't visited home even once. My heart weeps only for the puja room there. I miss only my *thakurghar.* That was the room where I sat with my ma-in-law. I was just an eight-year old bride, a creature of *gauri-daan*; she taught me all the little nitty-gritties of worshipping, it felt like playing a game. I didn't tell my daughters before leaving – Uma-Roma would've jumped up and down in rage. They would have stopped me if they knew. I told my son and daughter-in-law, I'm leaving, but no, I do not wish to die in a rented space. The moment I know that death's on my doorstep, I'll promptly return to this home of your forefathers. No dear, no matter how troublesome that may be for you, Nistarini won't breathe her last in a rented place. This house still belongs to me. Just remember that. Okay? My daughters have come to know. And what a *Lanka-kanda* they created! Yesterday, Umi-Romi both came – the two pretty, young, graceful housewives who came with fruits and sweets, – when you were showing me the sunset, my dear, those were my Umi-Romi. They were adamant about taking their mother back. They said, 'If not in Rambagan, live in a separate house. (By God's grace I've no shortage of houses!) But not here. This is like a mess boarding of the office babus!' But even if I have houses, they're all on rent. Only one flat has fallen vacant at Park Street. There too, you go up and down on a lift as in here. My girls said go and stay there. The deposit, meaning the twenty-five thousand that I paid, that can be recovered, no problem. My elder son-in-law is a famous advocate in the High Court, earning millions – no place to hide the money – if the deposit money's not refunded, he'd make them forget their forefathers' blessed names for sure! Yes! We know how to recover our dues! But I told them, I quite like it here, I feel far more peaceful out here. Why live alone, all by myself in the Park Street flat? Won't see a single face other than Mokkha-da's. Many more elderly ladies like me stay here, they are from very good families, from aristocratic backgrounds, how different they all are. Nice to see them. If they can stay here, why can't I? Are they from the rubbish bin? And is Nistarini Queen Victoria or what that she'll find it hard to stay in the home for the aged? I have no problem here at all. Timely meals, timely bath, a time for chatting and gossiping. My puja? I can finish that in my room itself. And that south-facing verandah! Oh, that verandah will never let me return to Rambagan! How many times can water change colours in a day? Would I've ever known these wonderful things in my life? Have I ever seen all this?

The other day, the didi from room number six, that Brahmo lady, some kin of Rabi Thakur, I believe, she told me, didi, I keep on gazing at the water all day long, and still can't have enough of it, my eyes don't seem to be satisfied – their thirst is never quenched, I long to see more, such infinite variety, this glimmer of light-water-sunbeam-colour, pure divine playfulness, she said. Can I use language as beautifully as that didi from room number six can? I'm just an illiterate woman and she's a learned school-teacher. I've been around in this world for such a long time, yet it feels as though my eyes were tightly shut through all these years. Her words opened the closed windows of my eyes. Now I'm learning to see. I see more and more each day. There's no end to what one can see. From the roof of Rambagan house, one saw only more roofs and more houses. The lovely greenery, the picturesque water of the lake, the wide, wide sky – will I get all these there? Living in a small place makes the mind small too, didi. It's good that I came away in a huff. There's so much to learn even in your old age! I'm learning something new every day. Look, how I'm learning to crochet, to knit laces, in my old age? Oh my eyes are sharp as a hawk's – no, no, there's no trace of cataract or any such thing, thank you! After coming here I've listened to lectures too. Famous persons visit us in the Hall downstairs – and the good things they say! Famous singers come to sing, writers come to read their stories and poems, famous

teachers lecture on different subjects. Never attended
a school in my life; but after coming here, I get a funny
feeling, as if I've joined a boarding school! Truly, didi, I
don't want to return to Rambagan Lane any more. Let
Tutu and Bouma live a long and happy life wherever
they may be, every day I pray to god for them. He's the
only remaining light of my life. I don't want to create
trouble for him and shorten his life-span. He'll have no
problem with his wife any more. His wife is very keen
to move away to the posh Park Street flat. My loyal son
says, 'How can I leave Ma here and go away elsewhere?'
His wife believes that the Rambagan neighbourhood
is only for the uncultured. Civilized people don't live
there. 'If you live here, I won't live with you', she
tells him. But how could poor Tutu leave his mother?
The situation was becoming seriously complicated.
Now I am thinking of giving away the key to the Park
Street flat to Tutu. Let him be free to go, let him shift
there, if he wants. Actually it will be Kanto and his
wife who'll stay put at Rambagan and look after the
ancestral property. That wife of Tutu's will neither take
care of my Kalachand nor light the lamp at the tulsi
plant every evening. But yes, my elder daughter-in-law,
Kanto's wife'll do that. Let Tutu move to Park Street.
Wherever they live in peace and harmony will be my
gain.

As long as Bishnukanto Bhattacharjee's son is alive, I've no worry about the Rambagan house. Tutu is my flesh and blood; Kanto's more than that to me. Bhattacharjee Moshai was Kanto's father. What he meant to me, to explain all that today – better to drop it, didi, that story is an old one, a worn out story, useless nonsense – it has no value for the people of today.

'Twilight Shelter' Ten — Geeta

Your father has gone out of his mind, I tell you. You can't say whatever you want and get away with it. Today you want to send your mother who showed you the world to the ashram; tomorrow you'll tell me to get lost. The person who can send his own mother away to the ashram, will he hesitate to throw his wife out? No, sir! That won't be allowed to happen here. There are problems? Let there be. A shortage of space? Let it be. As long as she lives, your mother stays in your house. That's all! Aren't you ashamed to even think of such things? We quarrel? Well, that's our affair. If you feel embarrassed, you go. Go and live happily in a hotel. What do you say, Monua? Your father's troubled by our screaming, tell him to go away. But why should grandma go? Today your father'll send away his mother who gave him birth; tomorrow, following in his footsteps, you'll send away your mother who bore you. No. That won't do. This house hasn't come to such a dire state of ugly misfortune that the mistress of the house must be sent out on the road to bring back its elegance! Tell me, my dear, is this why your widowed mother sold her ornaments and mortgaged her house to send you for your higher studies abroad? Did she spend five years cooking in her brother's house, for this end? Much learning you have acquired, honestly!

No. I don't want to see it. No matter how good the place is. Even if it's the Taj Mahal, after all it's someone else's house. Why must the old lady leave her own familiar place in her old age? Didn't she have her own house before? She lost it – because of you! No, I can't support such an immoral act, being a mother of children myself. To live happily with husband and children after getting rid of the mother-in-law – whoever does that, let them do it – I won't stop them, but do not ask me to do it. I cannot give this lesson to my son, that when parents grow old and aren't able to help in the family any more, they should be chased away like crows? Let the old woman be, she's busy with her own puja rituals. We quarrel? Yes, we do. So? People quarrel only with their own. Having lived together since my marriage, for all these twenty-five years, can't we at least quarrel?

You're embarrassed, so you have to send your mother away? Why? Can't wait unless you occupy her room, is that it? That big verandah isn't big enough to seat your clients, is it? Since the room is small and easy to air-condition, you want to shift your mother from there. You think I don't understand anything? Let the clients not have an air-conditioned room to sit in. Ma stays in her own room. This is her household. I'm her daughter-in-law. Whose household is this? Yours? Who chose me carefully and brought me here? To be the daughter-in-law of this family? Was it you? You were in England then. You accepted the bride your mother had selected for you, without a second thought, such was your trust in your mother. And now that you've made some money, your mother has become a burden? With a little more money, your wife too will become a burden. Instead, why not move into a bigger flat? You won't need to rob mother of her room then. But will you ever get your mother back once she's gone? Is this the wisdom with which you wear your gown and fight your cases? Can't understand why clients come to you at all! Let's go, Monua, and stop this talk. It's time for grandma to return from your aunt's place. Will she live here if she hears of this? Terribly stubborn, sentimental, and proud is that old grandma of yours. Take care that she doesn't hear a whisper of this. Really, what a matchless child her womb gave birth to!

Aparajita's Narrative

It's time for the chariot to reverse. The other side of life's experience is old age. Our entire life is driven by attraction, sheer attraction. It is on the other side that one meets the opposite force, a pull in the opposite direction. Here, there is no yearning to possess, no hurry to give either. The mind scales a strange plateau of solitude where the sharp feelings of joy and sorrow have both mellowed down.

Love for one's own children? Yes, that may be the only feeling that endures. The pull of the umbilical cord coils around, the only force that still retains the power to pierce us with needle-sharp pain. If anything happens to my sons I shan't be able to bear it. Humanitarian feelings have gradually shrunk and finally taken shelter in the animal instincts of motherhood. All other bonds have loosened and fallen away. No obstacles, no inhibition of the tongue will stop me from saying, 'Open the exit door.'

[*Note:* All the poems quoted in this section are by Rabindranath Tagore.]

A strange dusky glow bathes the mind, the intellect and the consciousness. The mind begins its return journey.

I am on my way
Where there are no names
Where all details cease
To be and not to be merged into one
Where the day is unbroken,
Without light without darkness

Really! The poet is unique. How beautifully he has thought. He could have easily said 'unbroken night'? But no, its the 'unbroken day'. When 'that which lies veiled within the golden vessel' is revealed, how can there be night? Quite true. The question of light and dark will wither away beyond that point. Only clarity remains. Only the infinite, the indivisible, the doubtless endures.

Just the opposite of mortal life. As long as there is life, there is uncertainty. Infinite, persistent doubt. As experience grows, doubt grows as well. Old age does not free us of uncertainty. It does not assist faith, does not strengthen its arms. Instead, as I have observed in my life, doubts increase with age, and the old answers become unacceptable. Is friction-free peace to be found anywhere?

The sun of the first day had asked
At the first appearance of Being
Who are you?
There was no answer.

It is no wonder that the poet wrote such bitter words during the last stages of life.

You have enmeshed the path of your creation
In traps of strange deceits, oh Deceitful One!

Today I realize what despair and dejection brought forth such lines from the poet. Had there been an 'ocean of peace stretched out' before him, would he have written those lines? The endless ocean of peace is a utopian dream, the finite's prayer for eternity, just a desperate desire. That's all.

From this wheelchair, I watch the sun's first appearance, playfully lifting the blood red veil of dawn. Then again, the sun's second round of colourful flirtation with the dusk. Seated in this chair I write letters, read, listen to music, converse with guests, meditate in solitude, pray. The prayer room, the parlour, the library – this chair is everything, all in one. What more do I need? But I am not bored. I spend time chatting with visitors every day. I propel my chair into the lounge to watch the news on TV, or plays, and films if there is a good one showing. I deliberately avoided installing a TV in my room so that I don't become too self-contained. I wouldn't feel like propelling my chair to the lounge then. The sense of pain is a bodily matter. Thank goodness that the disease hasn't affected my mind. Hasn't affected my speech. This girl takes good dictation. I write every day through her.

The Voice of Being. *Asti godavari tire vishaal shalmali taru* – By the river Godavari stands an immense shalmali tree – that shalmali tree was a tender plant once. Actually nothing is lost. No one disappears.

A long time ago, the little girl with kohl-lined eyes who was playing hopscotch in the courtyard at the dawn of her consciousness, she still moves about among the crowd – her eyes reflecting the surprise of fresh discoveries, her soft feet tripping in spontaneous dance. Yes, there she is on the shore, still there, the young adolescent and the fully blown young woman, whose riches make you envious.

And here?

A great shalmali tree has grown here, with limbs stretched out in all directions, cleverly hiding its essential being behind itself.

Through the tough crocodile skin of its branches, I can still glimpse the vanished moments of childhood, adolescence, and youth, playing hide and seek with their fresh young bodies; I can hear the rising notes of their soft laughter, I can clearly hear the voice of my being.

What surprises in the last phases of one's life! What novelty! Familiar people have become unfamiliar. New people. Me, too, am a stranger. Only to them? Am I not a stranger to myself as well? I could not be what they wished me to be, what they expected. As parents have expectations of their children, children too have unarticulated expectations from their parents. Disappointed children, like disappointed parents, also become disheartened. That's natural. So, it is better to step out now. My intuition is very powerful. I have some finer abilities that can grasp things beyond the senses. Like the dog's sense of smell, our Creator has granted me a sixth sense, an instinctive power, a keen, sharp, intuition. My son is just the opposite. He takes after his father. He can't differentiate between a person's basic intentions and her external behaviour. I can. Her husband never understood my daughter-in-law's inner feelings. He only heard what she uttered and acted accordingly. But I can clearly see the shape of her unspoken, inner desire. And act appropriately. That's why mother-in-law and daughter-in-law could live in one household without dissension. And the reason for my coming here – that upset my stupid son so much – also lies there. This way I am free. And so are they. It would have been difficult for me to live with those unfamiliar people and they too would have had problems adjusting to the new person that I am today. How can anyone be relaxed with a terminally ill patient at home? The entire household is disrupted. Waiting.

> This is better. Living in the same city.
> The doors will remain open,
> both the entrance and the exit.
> You are free to leave when its time to go.
> Come back again if you so wish.

I am experiencing memory lapses these days. What is the point of living on any longer? I have always lived independently. I wish to die independently as well.

Nistarini's Narrative

Hey, who's there? Aw, that you Umi? Romi too? Come on in! But why come again today my darlings? So soon? Can't wait to take Ma home? Is that it? And why so much sweet, child? However, my mind feels somewhat better today, yesterday was a very bad day. That nice didi in the room next to mine, with the name of the Aparajita flower, she wasn't well at all. Her son and daughter-in-law came and took her away yesterday, for

treatment in a good hospital in England. Some uncle of
the daughter-in-law is a big doctor there. Who knows
whether she'll ever come back? With the deadly disease
that she has! But she was such a nice person. No trouble
to anybody, sitting all alone by the window, busy with
her studies, writing with pen and paper the whole day.
Wonder what she wrote so much? When she took leave
she told us, 'If I come back, I will come back here.' But
will she ever come back?

Well, yes. Everyone has to go; some go early, some
late. My time will come too. This woman who's your
mother, who gave you birth, is she immortal? You've
come, that's good. Send word to Baro Bauma, inform
Kanto, and tell Puntey Chakkotti to fix a date. I must
finalize the papers, and divide up the property. Here
today, gone tomorrow ... it's better to finish signing
the documents. Better not delay it any more. I've
worried myself long enough over business and property
matters, from the day I took the first lessons from my
father-in-law about taking care of a business, and I've
had no respite ever since. But not any more, children,
now you take what's yours. I'll give enough to you
all, but listen dearies, I want to leave something for
these old women. At least one good house. And some
money. That house on Ballygunj Circular Road will be
good – it has a nice garden. My heart is really full here.

There should be more ashrams like this, more places for the old people, that's what I fancy. Speaking about the Choudhurys of Rambagan, aren't their vessels of sins too full already? May be the load will lessen a bit by setting up such ashrams. The family survived with Nistarini's help; now Nistarini will give a facelift to all their fourteen generations. I'll die a happy woman if I see the ancestral home as an ashram. Oh, don't take me back to Rambagan, my darlings, instead, ask *Baro Jamai* to get this job done quickly. Try for that, my darling ones, if you want me to be at peace, do not pester me with the 'Come home, Ma, Come home, Ma' song! I'm fine here. What's there for me at home? What will I do there? But here, is it just one single life? An isolated existence here? No. So many lives are being lived side by side, one life mingles with the other, like waves of the seven seas. All care for one another, we watch one another and understand. Understand from within. Look, how very depressed we all were for the didi who left us yesterday? But today we are all feeling somewhat better. In this vast universe, is there just one game that the Creator plays with us? The more I see, the better I understand – Dear God, your Nistarini is infinitely blessed by you!

Today, everybody is feeling happy. I'll tell you why. That school-teacher woman who used to live there on the second floor? That pale, thin, all dried up female, with a stick like figure? Never mixed with anybody, never came to watch TV. She only went to the library to take out books or to the music room to listen to music. Buried herself in the corner, sulking, feeling sorry for herself. After both her parents died, she was on the road with a kid brother at the age of sixteen. Lucky she had passed her Matric that very year. That sixteen-year old girl found a teaching job, and worked continuously till a little over a year ago. Didn't stray to the wrong path. Brought up the baby brother with love and care, by teaching at a school. Just sixteen years old, imagine! That too an orphan! And with fair skin. Didn't she have to be wary of the lust of men? That girl worked to death for the sake of her brother, didn't even marry.

The new school-teacher who's recently come here, she isn't married either, quite old herself, said she has known that Shobha *didimoni* for a long time. She took a lot of trouble educating her brother, put him through school and college, found him a job. The brother became an ardent party-worker and soon an MLA at a pretty young age. Very famous, gets his pictures in the papers all the time.

She sent the brother to study, on the one hand, and studied herself on the other. Is that easy? And working full-time too. Became a graduate. Then got her brother married at the right age, the wife works in an office. They have two children.

This sister spent the money she had spilt her blood for, to buy a home in Garia – home meaning a flat in a big building. In her brother's name. Till then all was fine. The two of them, brother and sister, with the brother's wife, lived in the same home, ate in the same kitchen. But no sooner than she retired, the brother's wife brought her out and put her here. She said, the children were growing up and the flat was too small. No school now, so let her spread her limbs and live here comfortably. Need a room for the boy, a room for the girl. The very sister-in-law for whom your husband has a place in the world today, you throw that person out of your household? Why? For some extra space? The teacher woman is a quiet person, not the trouble-making sort at all. Had she been like this Nistarini here, then I'd have understood, yes. Was there no way other than chasing her out of her home? But this woman? She has no fight left in her. Sometimes she used to sit on her bed and shed tears silently, the other boarders said. The sister-in-law earns money. She pays two hundred and fifty rupees for her every month. A three-bedded room, that's cheap. The second floor is for the cheap rooms, you see?

The sister-in-law comes to meet her too, bringing home-cooked food, pretending as though she loves her so much. But through this one-and-half years, the brother hasn't come even once to meet his sister. The sister-in-law

comes alone, all dressed up. No one has laid eyes on the
brother. When asked, the wife says, 'He's busy, away in the
village, on tour.' One day the teacher woman had smiled
and commented, 'He won't come even if he's in town. I
know my brother. He didn't want me to come here.' We
know that the brother says nothing to the wife. He accepts
whatever the wife does. Their children are twenty-two or
twenty-three years old, so they must've been married a
while. That he eats from his wife's hand, means that the
wife is a virago. She controls the MLA, like a sheep.

But today, all of a sudden the strangest thing
happened. The schoolteacher's niece – Maitri or Gayatri
her name is – has passed engineering. The brother's kids
used to come to meet their aunt sometimes. After passing
engineering, that girl has got a good job somewhere near
Delhi. Got residential quarters there also, it seems. Today
she came, got her aunt released, and just took her away
with her to Delhi. The schoolteacher woman distributed
sweets to us. She couldn't hold back her tears. I don't
know how to put it, Umi-Romi, that girl told us to the
face, 'It was *Pishimoni* who brought up our father from
the time he was eight. The day mother brought her here,
that day I had promised Pishimoni, as soon as I stood
on my own feet I would bring her back. I'd not let her
live like in a *banabas*, exiled for the rest of her life. I've
told my mother clearly, "Ma, when you retire, shall we

also send you away to the ashram? Shall I book a room there and keep it ready?"' While she was talking to us, her Pishimoni was packing her bags and soaking her sari with tears. I stood open-mouthed listening to that young girl. Isn't this country changing! Tiny twenty or twenty-two year-old slip of a girl, speaking like that, could we ever think of such things?

Look, Umi-Romi, there's everything in this world. If there's a Rambagan, there's also Dakhshineswar-Belur. That's why I feel that had I never come here, I would have known only one side of this vast life, only the rough tough seamy side of experience. Here, I can see the other, softer side, the finer side with the careful embroidery. Human life – can it be only of one kind? I'm seventy and yet it's like going through my *annaprashan*, tasting the first morsel of food. Nistarini has found her *nistar*, her release at last. I'll write off the business, and that's it. Freedom! Mother, you've at last let me out of Rambagan Lane! On this day, every one is happy. Children may say many things when they're hurt. But that she would remember what she had promised in school, after passing her exams, really get a job, and come back to take her old aunt out of this cowshed – her aunt had never imagined that it could happen.

But no, I'll not call this place a 'cowshed'. That barrister's wife – no, the judge's wife – whatever, that one, that crone who keeps her face painted white with powder like a lime-washed broken wall? Wears blouses showing her armpits, and wraps silk saris around in the modern style, and loiters around like the girls on the street of Rambagan and talks big? She calls this place a 'cowshed'. But doesn't that make you a cow yourself? Don't you have even that much sense? How many houses she had in Kolkata everybody knows. Only three! And not one is left. How many do I own? That too is not unknown to the residents here. But do I roam around looking like a clown? Act your age, I always say. When I was young, I dressed up, for sure, oh yes! But now? Dress to suit your age. Does she have any good sense? No dear, I don't call this place a 'cowshed'. Instead, this is like a school. A boarding school. Like Tutu's, in Darjeeling. This is a nice place. An excellent place. All are of similar age, like students in the same class. Is learning only of one kind? There are so many different kinds. Since I came to the 'Twilight Shelter', there's been no end to my learning. Aha, I say let her be happy, God bless her, let her be happy all through her life, that little engineer girl. Aha, people like her make the world go round, make the sun and moon rise. What's a child for? Thank goodness that the helm of the world is still in the hands of good people like her. That's why the vessels full of sin don't sweep the earth away, don't sink the three worlds. Why is this miserable heart so full of attachment? No release, even after leaving home and coming here! Whenever I think that I'll have to go away someday, leaving this world behind, my heart trembles. Who knows what lies there on the other side? Is there anything at all? Yet, this tattered, moth-eaten human life seems like a Kashmiri *jamawar* shawl, the older it gets, the more precious it becomes!

Glossary

adda	relaxed meeting and debating among friends
Akshay Tritiya	third day of the first month of the Bengali calendar, an auspicious day to start doing something new
alta	liquid red dye to outline the feet; worn by Hindu women
anchal	the outer end of the sari, has a multipurpose use
annaprashan	the ritual of feeding the baby her first grain of rice
Aparajita	also the name of a rare blue or white flower on a creeper, means unvanquished

arrey	exclamation of surprise
ayah	woman attendant
baburchi	chef
baiji	a courtesan trained in classical music
banalata	reference to Banalata Sen, a famous poem by Jibanananda Das; the lines on p. 14 of the novella are quoted from there
baniya	the trader caste in Kolkata, traditionally rich, but not a culturally advanced group
baro	big, elder
bouma	daughter-in-law
banabas	forest exile
Baro Jamai	elder son-in-law
batasa	sweets made of sugar or molasses used in puja
baithak khana	formal drawing room in the outer section of the house
Begumbahar	a fine cotton sari woven by expert weavers
beli	a fragrant white flower of spring and summer
Belur	Belur Math, monastery established by Swami Vivekananda for the followers of Ramakrishna Mission

Benda (Brinda)
  sakhi   a companion of Radha on her
                   rendezvous with Krishna, a term
                   used abusively here

Beyan   *behan*, mother of the bride, or groom
                   (*behai*, father), a honorific-marking
                   kinship used mutually between the
                   parents of the bride and the groom

bhai phota   *Bhratri Dwitiya*, a ritual observed by
                   sisters to bless their brothers with a
                   long life

bhajan   prayer songs

buri   old woman; used maliciously here

bordi   eldest sister

birthing Chember traditional Hindu homes have a spe-
                   cial room for 'birthing'

chaturmasya naam

  gaan   ceremonial singing in praise of the
                   deity through four rainy months at
                   a stretch. Vidyavachaspati Pandit
                   Madhusudan Ojha poetically
                   describes in *Kadambini*, his treatise
                   on meteorology, the process of
                   rainfall as the relationship of *megha-
                   malika* (line of clouds) and *nimitta*
                   (cause) leading to the conceiving

and delivery of a child. The sky-woman holds the embryo of rain conceived by sun-rays. The delivery of the child is the rainy season or chaturmasya

chhor-di	youngest elder sister
chhoto	small, younger
chhattu	gram flour
champa	a golden-coloured fragrant flower
Dakhshineshwar	famous Kali temple where Sri Ramakrishna used to worship
Dante's *Inferno*	The first part of Dante Alighieri's three-part Christian epic poem *Divine Comedy* – Hell, Purgatory, Paradise
darwan	sentry
debottar	debatra – property legally dedicated to the gods, and unavailable to the mortal inheritors of the rest of the property
didi	sister
didimoni	form of addressing a school-teacher
Dharma	religion, faith, morals. Also the Hindu deity of human ethics. Refers to the Mahabharata. Dharma came disguised as a crane to test the

	Pandavas, only Yuddhishthir passed his tests
elachidana	small grainy white sugar candy containing a cardamom seed inside, used as offerings in puja
esraj	a stringed instrument
Gandhiji	Mohandas Karamchand Gandhi
Ganga jal	water from Ganga that purifies
gauri-daan	giving away of a child bride by the age of eight in the manner, as Puranas describe, Gauri was married to Shiva
Gita, Bhagavat	Hindu scriptures
ghomta	covering head and forehead by using the end of the sari like a veil
gurudeb	a male spiritual mentor
guruma	a female spiritual mentor
Harir loot	showering of batasa, elachidana, and coins, as prasad, in the name of Hari, among devotees
ilish	hilsa, salt water fish greatly relished by Bengalis
jamaibari	son-in-law's house [bari = house]
Jagannath	Lord of the World, as Krishna appears in the temple at Puri
Jibanananda Das	one of the most important poets of modern Bengal

Kashi-Vrindaban	Varanasi and Vrindavan, places of pilgrimage where old and young Hindu widows from Bengal used to be exiled
Kabishekhar	an honorific for the Bengali poet Kalidas Ray
kafri	African
keya, ketaki	monsoon flowers with strong aroma, blossoming on thorny bushes
kadam	kadamba, fragrant monsoon flowers, which blossom on the kadamba tree that is famous as the tree under which Krishna played the flute for Radha in Vrindavan
Kalachand	The Dark Moon: a name for Vishnu or Krishna as a family deity
khoka	boy, common form of addressing a male child
Kashmiri jamawar	highly prized intricately embroidered shawl made in Kashmir, very precious and rare these days
kherestan	derived from *khrishtan* for Christian
khus-khus	an aromatic plant used as a scent and a cooling agent in summer
kunjaban	woods where Krishna played with gopikas or the milkmaids of

	Vrindavan; here, profanely, a meeting place for lovers
Lanka-kanda	The 'Sundar Kanda' of the Ramayana, where Hanuman sets fire to Lanka, an expression used to describe any disastrous situation
MLA	Member of the Legislative Assembly
Mamima	maternal uncle's wife (maternal uncle = mama)
Masima	mother's sister
Meshomoshai	masima's husband
moshai	an honorific for gentleman
matsyamukhee	a ritual of tasting fish ending the period of grieving and abstinence when death rites are over, establishing normalcy by returning to a non-vegetarian diet
mlechcha	non-Hindu, outsider, impure
morha	cane furniture, a small seat
Morarji	Morarji Desai, famous politician and former Prime Minister of India, well-known for preaching urine therapy
Manoj Basu	noted Bengali writer
nistar	reprieve
paan	betel leaf, chewed with tobacco as a luxury

panchabyanjan	an elaborate meal with at least five courses
Parsi border	a specialty of the Parsi community, beautifully hand-embroidered borders that can be attached to saris
pishima	father's sister
pishimoni	a fond way of addressing pishima
prasad	offerings to the deity, distributed among devotees after the worship
Premendra Mitra	famous Bengali writer
pronam	obeisance, touching one's elders' feet
purdah-nasheen	women kept behind the curtain
puja	worship
pujo special	special annual numbers of literary journals published in Bengal during the Durga Puja
Purabi	an evening raga
Puri-Digha-Gopalpur	popular seaside resorts; Puri and Gopalpur are in Orissa, while Digha is in West Bengal
rabri	an expensive delicacy, a sweetened, thickened milk dish
Rambagan, Sonagachi	well-known red light areas in Kolkata

Rabi Thakur	Rabindranath Tagore
safeda	a sweet fleshy and juicy fruit (Sapodilla)
Samar Sen	noted Bengali poet
Samaresh Basu	famous Bengali novelist
Sankataharan	remover of all danger; a name for god
sindur	vermillion in the parting of the hair is a sign of marriage for a Hindu woman
shalmali	(*Salmalia malabaricum*) *shimul* or silk cotton tree with wide spreading branches and crimson flowers
shiuli	shefali, a fragrant flower with delicate white petals and orange stalk, that blossoms after the monsoons, in early autumn
sthitadhee	settled in one place in equanimity; motionless as in meditation
sulking chamber	*gosa ghar* in tales, where queens shut themselves up to express anger, like the wilful queen Kaikeyi sulked to pressurize her husband King Dasharath in the Ramayana
surbahar	a stringed instrument
surma	kohl
thakur	deity, also, father, patriarch, and father-in-law

thakurdalan	a hall attached to the *thakurghar*, the puja room, a place of worship
thakurghar	room for the deity
thakurpo	literally, father-in-law's son; honorific for the husband's younger brother
upanayan	ritualistic investiture of the sacred thread for Brahmin boys during their adolescence, marking their second birth and formal initiation into Brahminism
vanaprastha	the Vedas expound the wisdom of experiencing human life in four ashrams or stages: *brahmacharya*, the stage of learning and self-control; *grahasthya*, experiencing family life; *vanaprastha* or leaving for the forest to meditate upon and prepare for the final stage; *sannyasa* or ascetic life
vanaprasthee	one who practises vanaprastha
zari	golden thread

About the Author and the Translator

Author

NABANEETA DEV SEN was born in Kolkata, West Bengal. She is a creative writer, an academic, and a scholar-critic. Her academic and critical analyses are in English, and creative writings in Bengali. She retired as Professor of Comparative Literature, Jadavpur University, Kolkata, and has more than eighty publications including poetry, novels, short stories, travelogues, translations, memoirs, essays, besides children's literature. She is the recipient of many awards, including the 'Padma Shree'. She says 'How do I know who I am until I have written myself and read myself on a piece of paper in front on me? ... Poetry has been my *kabach-kundal* – my charmed amulet, my magic armour ...'

Translator

TUTUN MUKHERJEE was born in Dhanbad, Bihar (now Jharkhand). She is Professor at the Centre for Comparative Literature and Joint Professor at the Centre for Women's Studies and the Department of Theatre Arts, University of Hyderabad. She has translated and edited eleven volumes of plays, short stories, novellas, and criticism. Her publications include: *Translation: From Periphery to Centrestage; Mindscapes: Short Stories of Premendra Mitra; Staging Resistance: Plays by Women in Translation.* She has also translated *Five Novellas by Women Writers* and *Twilight of the Mind: Selected Short Stories of Baig Ehsas.*